A Reluctan

By John Pilkington

© John Pilkington 2022.

John Pilkington has asserted his rights under the Copyright, Design and Patents Act, 1988, to be identified as the author of this work.

First published in 2022 by Sharpe Books.

TABLE OF CONTENTS

ONE	1
TWO	14
THREE	27
FOUR	39
FIVE	51
SIX	64
SEVEN	75
EIGHT	86
NINE	98
TEN	110
ELEVEN	123
TWELVE	136
THIRTEEN	149
FOURTEEN	162
FIFTEEN	175
SIXTEEN	185

ONE

Revill was nearing the end of his tether.

Perhaps it was the October rain, which had soaked his cloak and hat, while the wet grass of the Artillery Yard was sending a chill up through his boots. Or perhaps it was the sight of the hundred and fifty bedraggled men of the trained-band under his charge, tramping dejectedly about the field. Or it might have been a memory of the hard words he'd had with Jenna in the early dawn, on account of his coming in somewhat drunk. Then again, perhaps it was none of these things, but plain boredom and a powerful desire for a pipe of tobacco. When his sergeant, Tom Bright, appeared at his elbow, he didn't even look round.

'Can't we call it a day, Captain?' Bright muttered, holding his old soldier's coat over his head. 'The men have done their drill. I find no fault with them, and I'm as cold as a witch's-'

'You see that sour-faced fellow over there?' Revill demanded, cutting him off. He jerked a thumb over his shoulder, towards a man standing near the archery butts, watching them.

'I do,' came the reply. 'Who is he, then?'

'I think he's one of the Aldermen hereabouts, looks to me like a Puritan down to his goose-turd stockings. If I call a halt too early, he'll likely report me from sheer meanness.'

'Someone you've offended?' The wiry little sergeant enquired, with a shiver. 'Sweet Jesus, if I had a crown for every-'

'You wouldn't be here,' Revill finished. 'And I haven't offended anyone.'

Bright pursed his lips. His old captain (nobody else called him that) could be a taciturn man at times. Then, nobody else save the sole surviving member of his artillery crew knew him as well as his old gun-layer did. As he knew that commanding one of the London trained-bands every week was no task for an officer like Will Revill, the most restless man he knew. At times, he wondered whether a return to the war in Flanders might be preferable to the dull life they had fallen into since coming home. Then Bright would start to remember what it was like – the bloody, blistering awfulness of it all - and curse himself for a fool who should be grateful he still possessed life and limb.

'And yet...' Revill turned to him abruptly. 'The rain's worsening. Anyone carrying a flask of powder would need to keep it dry, wouldn't they?'

'Well, they would,' the sergeant replied after a moment. 'And the calivers are getting wet... they'll need to dry the barrels out.'

'Indeed...' Revill met his eye and glanced towards the watcher, who hadn't moved.

'Shall I stroll over and have some speech with the alderman?' Bright suggested. 'I can say you're concerned for the men's weaponry, let alone the chance of them catching a chill.'

'You could do that,' Revill allowed. 'Tell him he can get a full report on their fitness from... from the Master of Ordnance, a firm friend of mine.'

A RELUCTANT ASSASSIN

'Are you sure you want me to say that? The Master hates you like the plague.'

'See now, I'll trust you to find the words, then I can dismiss the men. You'll find me in the White Hart by Bishopsgate, where I'll stand you a mug.'

'Ah... well, that'd help.' The sergeant's countenance brightened. Turning on his heel, he walked off towards the spectator. Revill watched him go, thinking that for an alderman of a populous ward like this, the fellow must have precious little to keep him occupied. Important though it was that the men were ready to defend London at all times, given the mayhem of last year, few would have stood in the rain to watch their pike-drill.

Turning to face the trained band, he realised that the drummer had stopped beating in time. The drumhead was wet, of course... coming to a decision, he raised his arm and brought the troop to a halt.

'That will serve, good citizens!' He called. 'The company is dismissed – get yourselves out of the rain and off home!'

There was an audible sigh of relief from the packed pikemen and those shouldering empty calivers, along with an outbreak of muttering, the kind common to soldiers of every sort. Doubtless the armies of Greece and Rome, and the Assyrians before them, had grumbled in the same way, Revill thought. Then, he had never seen much sense in drilling in tight formation, pikes poking above men's heads like the spines of a hedgehog. The companies made easy targets on the field of battle, where one well-aimed shot from a demi-cannon could wreak havoc among them... with a quick shake of his head, he dismissed such memories. He turned to see if Bright had finished his task, then saw the sergeant approaching him accompanied by

3

the watcher, his assumed alderman – who would turn out to be something quite different.

'Master Revill,' the man said, drawing to a halt. 'I thought you'd never bring the comedy to a close. I'd have sent this rain-sodden rabble home half an hour ago.'

Revill blinked, facing a stolid-looking man clad in a heavy cloak. 'You would, eh?' He met the other's eye defiantly. 'Then, I'll wager you're not captain of a trained-band. I'm tasked with keeping the men of Bishopsgate Ward up to scratch. There's a war on, last I heard.'

'True,' the other returned. 'And I heard you were up to your neck in it until a few months back. I won't ask who you bribed to get leave to come home… wounds or no.'

'Do I know you?' Revill enquired. 'If you wanted to speak to me, why didn't you do so sooner?'

'Privacy,' was all the stolid man said. He glanced pointedly at Tom Bright, who had remained tight-lipped.

'My sergeant stays,' Revill said at once.

A short silence followed, before the other nodded. 'Very well. My instructions were to bring you to the house of The Queen's Secretary, Sir Francis Walsingham, but you can make your own way there. Do you know where it is?'

'It's in Seething Lane…' Revill frowned. 'Are you sure you've got the right man?'

'Are you not Captain William Revill, who served under Lord Willoughby at the siege of Bergen-op-Zoom? Who captured a Spanish cannon, and turned it upon the enemy?'

'That he is, sir - and was mightily commended for it.'

It was Bright who spoke, with some resentment. The experience, barely a year ago, had bound the two of them like brothers ever since, not least because of the companions they had lost in that dreadful siege. When the questioner turned to look at him, he met his gaze without flinching.

'So I've heard – sergeant.' The messenger, as he now appeared to be, eyed him coolly. 'And I hold him in as much respect as you do. But if you were thinking to accompany your master to Seething Lane, you'll not be admitted. It's private business.' He faced Revill. 'I'm not privy to its nature. Can I trust you to proceed without further delay?'

'You can,' Revill answered, somewhat absently. It was only now sinking in that one of the most important men on Queen Elizabeth's council, indeed in the entire country, wanted to see him. Why that might be, he could not imagine.

'Then my task is done,' the messenger said. 'Though I'd tidy myself up a bit first, if I were you,' he added. 'You look like a drowned rat.'

And he was gone, striding off towards Hog Lane. Revill and Bright watched him go, whereupon the little sergeant gave a sigh of resignation.

'I suppose the White Hart will have to wait, then?'

Revill merely shrugged.

***

The walk from the Artillery Yard to Seething Lane, close to Tower Hill, took no more than a quarter of an hour. Instead of passing under Bishopsgate and threading their way through the teeming city, the two men turned the corner by the Dolphin Inn and tramped around the walls by Houndsditch to Aldgate. From there they walked down Poor Jewry into Hart Street, where Bright stopped outside the door of an alehouse. Away to the left, the great bulk of the Tower loomed ominously above their heads.

'I'll be in the tavern if you need me, Captain,' the sergeant said, jerking his head. 'I'll pass an hour or so, then if you don't come I'll get myself home.'

They were almost at the turning to Seething Lane, a quiet street of fine dwellings inhabited by men of status. Revill, who had been mulling over the possible reasons for his unlikely invitation to attend Master Secretary, came out of his reverie.

'That's well...' he fumbled for his purse. 'Either way, I'm standing you that mug.'

Bright took the coin with a nod and turned to go inside, while Revill resumed his steps. A short while later, he was giving his name to the gatekeeper of Sir Francis Walsingham's elegant, walled townhouse, and was admitted. But no sooner had he passed through the front doors, into an imposing hallway, than a sentry blocked his way.

'Sir Francis is too sick to see anyone,' he announced. 'Don't you listen to Court news?'

Revill gave his name, adding: 'I was ordered to attend him without delay, so here I am. The messenger didn't say what it was about.'

'And I'm telling you, no-one save his physician is being admitted,' the guard retorted.

A pause followed, during which Revill began to wonder if someone had played a particularly tiresome joke on him. It was common knowledge that Walsingham was often ill nowadays, with his kidney stone and various other ailments. Some said he was so exhausted by Crown business that he was ready to die. But then, the messenger at the Artillery Yard had seemed an unlikely prankster... he was summoning a reply when another man appeared from somewhere and hurried forward.

A RELUCTANT ASSASSIN

'Captain Revill?' This one said brusquely, moving up beside the sentry. He wore the dusty black gown of a clerk. 'You took your time, didn't you?'

'I came as soon as I received the message,' Revill answered. 'Now I'm told Sir Francis is gravely ill, so I confess I'm-'

'You're with me,' the clerk said.

Drawing the guard aside, he muttered a few words in his ear which Revill didn't catch. But the upshot was, the other nodded and stood back, allowing him to follow the busy official as he led the way across the hall and down a passage hung with tapestries. Soon they stood outside a door, whereupon the clerk knocked, lifted the latch and poked his head round. A voice spoke, and Revill was ushered inside - to stop in surprise. Seated at a table, with writing materials and neat stacks of papers, was a man he recognised at once.

'Master Chamberlain?' Somewhat awkwardly he made his bow, hearing the door close behind him. He was alone with no less a personage than the Queen's Vice-Chamberlain, Sir Thomas Heneage. Silently, he regretted ignoring the messenger's suggestion that he tidy his appearance.

'Revill.' The finely-dressed courtier, in his late fifties and a man of considerable presence, favoured him with a thin smile. 'I see you've had a trying walk... would you care to dry yourself?'

He rose from his chair and gestured to where a good sea-coal fire burned, at which Revill nodded. Soon the two of them were standing before the blaze, though Heneage maintained a discreet distance. Having put off his hat and cloak, though his mind was busy with questions Revill, managed to remain silent.

'I saw you in Flushing, three years ago,' Heneage said affably. 'Someone pointed you out as a most worthy, if somewhat intemperate officer.'

Revill gave a polite nod.

'Though of course, a lot of water has flowed under the bridge since then,' the other continued. 'As it flowed at Bergen when they opened the dykes, I heard. Still, for a casualty of war, a drowned Spaniard is as good as one who's been shot... wouldn't you agree?'

Revill returned his gaze. It had crossed his mind - somewhat optimistically, he now thought - that he might have been called here to be given some sort of promotion, or a commission to return to the Low Countries. Now, he wondered if he was in trouble for some reason. He had tensed, realising that his wet clothes were steaming, and raising an odour that he hoped the Vice-Chamberlain wouldn't notice.

'It's war, sir,' he answered finally. 'The King of Spain's commanders don't scruple to use all possible means to achieve their ends, so why should we?'

'Precisely so,' Heneage agreed. 'And if I've heard correctly, you seldom bothered with scruples yourself... at the capture of Axel, in particular.'

At that, Revill drew a breath; he had no wish to be reminded of the brutal slaughter of the defenders of that doomed little town, once the siege had been broken. 'I was there,' he admitted. 'But I put no man to the sword who wasn't threatening me. It's true some of our troops were enraged... made mad by the loss of their comrades, hence-'

'Yes, yes.' Heneage made a dismissive gesture. 'I don't need to hear your soldiers' tales.'

'Then forgive me, sir,' Revill replied, curbing his impatience. 'But I confess I'm at a loss to know why I'm

A RELUCTANT ASSASSIN

here. I was told to attend Sir Francis, only to find that he's unwell.'

'Master Secretary still works from his sick-bed, but he is limited,' came the other's reply. 'I'm taking on some of his duties, and it was expedient to be discreet. To come to the nub of the matter, Revill, I have a task for you... one that requires complete and utter discretion.'

'For me?' Revill blurted in surprise. Discretion was hardly a quality he was noted for; he could almost hear Tom Bright guffaw at the notion.

Heneage was watching him. In the silence, he found himself taking in the man's grey hair and grizzled beard, neatly-trimmed though it was. He found it hard to square this personage with the dashing young courtier who had once been a favourite of the Queen, and made the Earl of Leicester furiously jealous. Then, offices of state wore men down, aged them well before their time – and corrupted them too, he'd often thought.

'I need you to do me a service,' the Vice-Chamberlain said then, seemingly having settled on a decision. 'It's wholly secret, requiring a man of determination, as well as someone of wide resources. I think you would perform it well enough.'

'I'm honoured... if not flattered,' Revill said. He tried to ignore the feeling of unease that was stealing over him: one familiar to any soldier who was about to be handed an unpleasant assignment.

'Don't be,' Heneage replied, brisk on a sudden. 'The task is a once-and-for-all mission, for which you will be fittingly rewarded. But it isn't one to be relished. You should get it done swiftly, then return to London and forget about it.'

'Return to London?' Revill echoed. 'Where am I-'

'Into Surrey,' the other broke in. 'Farthingdown Manor, the seat of Sir Abel Stanbury, by the village of Weybridge.' He paused, then: 'You must snuff out his life.'

Revill stared, thinking he must have misheard.

'Not overtly, of course,' the other went on. 'You'll have to arrange a tragic accident. It shouldn't be too difficult. The man's as mad as a bedlamite fool, and clumsy as a blind bear. I leave it to you to find a suitable means. You needn't linger after that... just long enough to pay your condolences to the widow, and allay any suspicions.'

'Your pardon, sir.' Revill swallowed. 'I fear you're in error. I'm a soldier, not an assassin.'

'I know perfectly well what you are,' came the smooth reply. 'As I know you're fully capable of carrying out this charge I place upon you. You're a loyal Englishman. Don't you fear for the Queen's safety, after the vile plots and machinations that have been laid against her these past years? Do I need to remind you of Babington, say - let alone the Armada?'

'You do not,' Revill answered sharply. Thoroughly alarmed now, he was searching for a form of words by which to make his refusal. Kill Sir Abel Stanbury, a man he had never even heard of? It was absurd...

'I should make one thing clear,' Heneage added. 'It's not a matter of choice.'

'Indeed – sir?' Revill struggled to keep his composure. 'Well, I'm bound to disappoint you. I'm nobody's hireling, nor will I snuff out any man's life, as you put it, who has done me no harm.'

To that, Heneage let out a sigh. 'In truth, I half-expected you to answer in such a fashion,' he said mildly. 'So let me be plainer: you have no other course. Do you know why?' And when Revill merely frowned, he laid it forth.

A RELUCTANT ASSASSIN

'You have a young sister named Katherine, down in Devonshire... recently wed, I understand. Nothing untoward there – except that she's married one Gerard Randall, a Catholic. Worse, she's converted to the Roman faith - to please her new husband, no doubt. Rather touching... but poor timing in the present climate, wouldn't you say?'

On a sudden, a cold hand seemed to clutch Revill's heart. His beloved Kate, the only surviving daughter of his widowed mother, had always been his joy – and now his bane. A weak point, since her conversion; at once, he saw it.

'So, you mean to blackmail me,' he began – only for Heneage to stiffen at once.

'Have a care, sir,' he snapped. 'You're in no position to throw accusations about. Nor do I need to lay forth the consequences of your failure to carry out my instruction. As for refusing...' he gave a shrug. 'I think you know that would be very foolish indeed.'

His mouth tight, Revill turned to gaze into the fire. He knew that this was no idle threat. Heneage could easily arrange for Katherine and her new husband to be hounded for their Papism, accused of aiding priests or some such offence. They could be ruined, imprisoned – or even worse. His mind racing, he struggled to find some remedy, but saw none.

He looked up to find Heneage regarding him with raised eyebrows. 'You see how the land lies, I think,' he murmured.

A moment passed, then: 'This... Sir Abel Stanbury,' Revill said heavily. 'May I ask why you want him killed?'

'Well now... that's better.' The other nodded. 'In short, he's a walking powder-keg. No Papist, yet he swears murder and mayhem to Her Majesty when he's in his cups… a would-be-plotter, though he hasn't the brains. But others might use him, his connections – such as they are. The Queen can't abide him nowadays, which has unbalanced him in my view. In these times we cannot be too careful… even with regard to a minor country knight. Now, do you understand?'

'I suppose so,' Revill replied, his heart sinking to his boots. Just then, he would have given anything to be back at the Artillery Yard in the pouring rain.

'Good,' Heneage said brightly. 'Do you have questions?'

At that Revill hesitated, as something puzzled him. He was not so innocent as to believe that the Queen's devoted Councillors would quibble at using ruthless means to remove someone they regarded as a risk, in these troubled times. But Heneage was a pen-wielding Courtier… then a new thought sprang up. It was an open secret that Sir Francis Walsingham was the Queen's spymaster - and the Vice-Chamberlain, it seemed, was taking over many of his duties. So, was there some intelligence he wasn't sharing? He looked up, to see the man moving back to his table without waiting for an answer.

'I'm providing you with expenses,' he said as he sat down. 'You should leave soon – tomorrow, perhaps. It's a good day's ride.'

'One moment, sir.' Revill took a step towards him. 'What reason would I have to journey to this place… Farthingdown? I would surely arouse suspicion.'

'Ah yes, I should have said.' Heneage nodded again. 'You're sent by the Queen's Surveyor of Works – his name is Thomas Blagrave, in case you didn't know. You've been instructed to make an inspection of the manor, as a suitable stopping place on the Queen's summer progress next year. We'll furnish you with a letter of authority, which will

A RELUCTANT ASSASSIN

enable you to come and go about the manor as you please. The Stanburys will welcome you with open arms, I expect. Sir Abel will think the Queen's forgiven him – and his wife will probably fall at your feet.'

He opened a small casket on his table, drew out a purse and, without warning, threw it to Revill who managed to catch it.

'You should take a servant with you, for appearance's sake,' the Vice-Chamberlain added. 'Someone you can trust to keep his mouth firmly sealed. Do you have anyone in mind?'

Despite the sickly sensation that had stolen over him, Revill nodded.

'Then I think we're finished. When you return, simply leave a message for me here, stating that the inspection at Farthingdown was completed to your satisfaction. That's all I need.'

Heneage met Revill's eye without expression, whereupon he made his bow, retrieved his hat and cloak and headed for the door. He opened it, then paused to glance back, but the other had taken up a quill and was busy at his papers.

A few minutes later he walked into the alehouse in Hart Street and found Tom Bright nursing a mug at a table in the corner. For the sergeant, one look at his face was enough.

'I'll call the tapster,' he muttered.

TWO

They set out soon after daybreak, crossing the Bridge into Southwark under heavy clouds: Revill on his old warhorse Malachi, and Bright on a hired jennet. They carried packs, leather flasks of weak beer and little else, save a letter in Revill's pocket from the Queen's Surveyor of Works, which had been delivered to his lodgings, the previous evening, by messenger. After a few miles' riding, and not a word said, the sergeant cleared his throat.

'So, you mean to accost Sir Abel Stanbury,' he ventured. 'What's he done, then?'

'Nothing, as far as I know,' Revill replied shortly. 'It's Court business. Seems they can't spare anyone else just now.'

He looked away, knowing full well how lame it sounded. As he knew that, sooner or later, his shrewd little sergeant would start to form his own opinions. He felt sick at heart, and weighed down with a mixture of anger and shame, that he had been forced into carrying out such a terrible task - in effect, a murder. He couldn't possibly tell Tom Bright the true nature of his mission – or not yet, anyway. As for how it might be accomplished, he had no notion. His only comfort was a vague hope that Stanbury would turn out to be such an unpleasant man, let alone a danger to the Queen, it would be no great wrench to arrange his demise. And yet, he cursed himself for agreeing to it.

A RELUCTANT ASSASSIN

'Seeing as you've been at a loose end ever since we got back from Flanders?' Bright enquired, after a moment. 'All the more so, since your wounds mended?'

'Something like that.'

'Well, it seems a strange charge to lay upon a master of artillery,' the sergeant persisted. 'Let alone a humble cannoneer like me-'

'Can we not stow this chatter?' Revill broke in, more sharply than he intended. 'I want to make Mitcham by noon, and take dinner. Isn't it enough to be out of London for a while?'

'Perhaps, Captain,' Bright replied. 'Yet I'm puzzled as to why you're so glum about it.'

'I'm not glum,' Revill told him, to which his sergeant merely sighed.

Thereafter, the morning passed with little further discourse. They rode through Newington and Streatham, meeting carters and tradesfolk coming into London for the markets. Then they were deep into Surrey, its green hills and woods about them. Bright, grown unused to riding, grunted with discomfort at times, though his horse was sure-footed enough. For his master – since they were to pass as master and servant – it was bittersweet to ride Malachi this day. As a rule, he would have been as glad of the exercise as the horse clearly was. He regarded the pleasant scenery, thankful at least that the rain had held off. Finally, when he glimpsed the church spire of Mitcham ahead, he slowed his mount to a walk.

'I know you're uneasy, Tom,' he said at last. 'But I can't speak about my business with Stanbury, and there it is.'

Bright was silent.

'When it's over and done with…' he paused. 'When we're on our way home, I might say more.' He drew a breath. 'And afterwards, mayhap you'll want to quit my company. If you did, I'd understand.'

The sergeant turned in the saddle, a frown appearing. 'You truly believe so?'

'I fear so,' Revill answered.

Then he shook the reins, and urged Malachi to a trot.

At the inn in Mitcham, they took dinner while the horses were fed and watered. Bright was subdued, seemingly mulling over their conversation. Revill, meanwhile, puffing on his pipe, had at last turned his thoughts to Jenna, and the bitter farewell he had taken of her at dawn.

As always, she had known perfectly well that he was lying.

'Another of your escapades – or is it some soldier's prank?' She had demanded. 'Last time you rode off I didn't see you for a week. If I didn't trust Tom Bright's word, I might have thought you had a trull somewhere. Where are you going this time?'

'What does it matter?' Revill had replied. 'The army orders me to carry a message, that's what I do. We should be thankful I'm not taking ship to Flanders-'

'And would you even tell me if you were?' His paramour had thrown back. 'Just to save my worrying, as you used to say?'

In his mind's eye he saw her now, defiant in her righteousness, hands on hips in their tiny lodgings in Abchurch Lane, her green eyes ablaze. A Cornishwoman to the ends of her toes, in the London broiderers' community of which she was part, she was often assumed to be Welsh, or even Irish. It had always amused them both. 'Remember this, my Captain,' she had once said, after they'd first lain together. 'An Irish maid is only a Cornish maid who can swim.'

A RELUCTANT ASSASSIN

How many times since then, he wondered now, had he felt obliged to tell her an untruth? Like the time an old enemy of his had found out where he lived and, livid with rage, had caught him in an alley and tried to stab him. Revill had got the better of the man, leaving him lying in the runnel with a cracked skull, but not before receiving a gash to his right hand. In answer to Jenna's anxious queries, he had mentioned an accident at the fencing hall. And then, there was the burning question of how long his army pay was going to last. He had yet to tell her that it was almost spent.

With a sigh he lowered his pipe, took up his mug, and found Bright's gaze upon him.

'Been wondering what services you might need from me, Captain, once we get to this manor,' he said. 'Seeing as it's what you call Court business.'

'It's merely for appearance's sake,' Revill told him, surprised to find himself echoing Heneage's words. 'You can treat it as a holiday... take the air, gossip with the servants.'

'And how long will we be staying there, might I ask?'

'I hope it's no more than a few days, though I can't be certain.'

The sergeant pondered this, while Revill's spirits began to flag. For the past couple of hours, he had tried to construct an excuse for the grisly task which lay ahead of him, to the extent of picturing Sir Abel Stanbury as a villain with secret Papist leanings, bent on mischief, whom it was his duty to despatch. Now, he suspected that his fancies had run away with him. Sitting upright on a sudden, he drained his mug and gestured towards Bright's pot of ale.

'Are you done? We'd best ride on if we're to make Farthingdown by nightfall.'

The other eyed him briefly, then gave a nod.

That afternoon, rain clouds began to threaten. Making good pace, within an hour they had put Morden and Malden behind them and were riding through Long Ditton on the Chertsey Road. And quite soon, it seemed, the day was waning to dusk, and after a brief rest to water the mounts, they were nearing Esher. The crossed the Mole, riding faster now against the coming night, and at last the village of Weybridge loomed ahead, lights showing at the windows. Here the River Wey flowed into the Thames, and away to their right lay the Queen's palace of Oatlands, by the river. Revill drew Malachi to a halt while Bright, who had fallen behind, came up beside him. The horses stamped, blowing in the gathering chill.

'I forgot to tell you,' Revill said, somewhat wearily. 'If anyone asks, we... I, that is... I've been sent by the Queen's Surveyor of Works, to look over the manor. It's a routine inspection, and that's all you know.'

The sergeant met his eye, but said nothing.

'So...' his master pointed upriver. 'Stanbury's seat is but a mile or so further, I believe. I'll be mighty glad to get indoors and take supper – won't you?'

But still Bright gave no answer. Whereupon Revill turned away abruptly, dug his heels into Malachi's sides and urged him forward.

A short time later, they were riding through an archway into a stable yard lit by torches, with the great manor of Farthingdown, seat of the Stanburys, a dark mass against the louring sky.

As he dismounted, Revill felt the first raindrops on his face.

***

Supper that night, in a candlelit chamber while rain lashed the windows, was a curious affair. It was a surprise

A RELUCTANT ASSASSIN

for Revill to encounter Sir Abel Stanbury, one of the most unsettling men he had ever met. From their first meeting in the dim hallway, when he had greeted Revill warmly enough, the man had barely stopped twitching: a spasm, that contorted his face from time to time. But far more alarming was his propensity to shout a word aloud, without warning, or even relevance to the conversation. After a while, unsure how to respond, Revill met the eye of his hostess, Lady Gisela, who was seated at his end of the table.

'My husband has had his affliction since boyhood, sir,' she said, without troubling to lower her voice. 'It frightens some people, yet I assure you there's no harm. You'll grow accustomed to it.'

Revill nodded courteously. Lady Gisela was an elegant woman of middle years, with a faint air of weariness, dressed in a faded blue-and-lilac gown and wearing few jewels. The setting was handsome enough, however, as was the Stanburys' table, and it subdued him somewhat to be in noble company. Servants stood by the panelled walls, ready to fill his wine-cup. For the past decade or so he had lived among soldiers and grown used to rough ways. Now, in the guise of a Crown official on important business, with a servant of his own who had been despatched to the kitchens to dine in humbler surroundings, he found himself accorded the status he had almost forgotten he merited: that of a gentleman.

'Where's your home, then?'

The sudden, shouted question from Sir Abel Stanbury broke his thoughts like a whipcrack. He turned to the master of Farthingdown, who was frowning at him from the other end of the table: a hawk-nosed, grey-bearded man with piercing eyes, wearing an old-fashioned fur-trimmed gown. The only other occupant was the steward: a crabbed, bald-headed fellow whose name Revill had barely caught. This one, with eyes lowered, was busying himself at his dessert; no doubt his master's behaviour was familiar to him.

'My family hail from Devonshire, sir,' Revill said, raising his voice. 'Though I've not seen them for a while. My army service took me to the Low Countries…'

'Among Dutchmen?' Sir Abel barked. 'Is it true they have webbed feet?'

Revill put on a faint smile. 'That's a myth,' he replied. 'Though it's true much of the land is boggy. There are some who go on stilts to leap across the marshes, so I've heard.'

The other eyed him, then abruptly his face relaxed into a look of polite interest. Disconcerted by the rapid change in his manner, Revill returned his gaze.

'And now you serve the Queen's Surveyor of Works,' the knight said, taking up his silver cup. 'I knew Blagrave, once. How does he nowadays?'

'I would say he's quite well, sir,' Revill answered, concealing his discomfort. It had not occurred to him to find out anything about the man who was supposed to have sent him here. To his relief his host merely nodded, took a drink and changed the subject.

'I'm glad to have you look over Farthingdown,' he said. 'We would of course be honoured to receive Her Royal Majesty, should she choose to visit next year.' He turned to his wife. 'Would we not, madam?'

But Lady Gisela gave no answer. Revill caught the look that passed across her features, and sensed a wariness on her part – or was it even disapproval? Yet Sir Abel, it seemed, expected no answer, and was waving his cup in the air so that its contents almost spilled. Having regained

A RELUCTANT ASSASSIN

Revill's attention, he indicated the steward, who had yet to utter a word.

'Ashman will take you around my lands tomorrow,' he announced. 'Go where you will - peer into every cranny. There's no better guide to Farthingdown – is that not so?'

He gave a twitch, and then waited as did Revill, for Ashman to look up from his plate. Finally, after what seemed an eternity, he raised his eyes.

'I'd be honoured, of course, Sir Abel,' he said, in the scratchy voice of a scholar rather than the steward of a great house. Whereupon he turned his gaze on Revill... who stiffened.

Master Ashman, he saw, was not honoured at all; in fact, he looked displeased. Their eyes locked briefly, but it was enough: the man resented the imposition, and appeared to wish that this interloper from London had never come here.

Revill kept expression from his face, and returned his gaze to Sir Abel.

'I too am honoured, sir,' he said. 'But can you not spare the time to accompany me yourself? I would like to know the history of your house.'

At that the steward grunted something inaudible, prompting Lady Gisela to speak.

'If my husband is well enough, and if the rain ceases, it may be that he'll venture out,' she said quickly, her eyes on Revill. 'But I dare say you'll ascertain the condition of Farthingdown soon enough – as you will judge its worthiness for a royal visit. Master Ashman will answer all your questions. Now, will you take more Hippocras?'

She beckoned to a footman, who came forward at once. But Revill put a hand over his cup and murmured a polite refusal. On a sudden, he had a desire to quit the table and get himself to the chamber he knew was prepared for him.

He was forming the words, when a shout from the other end made him start.

'To the devil with Hippocras!' Sir Abel cried. 'To the devil with everything!'

Revill followed Ashman's example in fixing his eyes on his plate.

***

By the next morning the rain had ceased, giving way to autumn sunshine. For Revill, however, the day brought surprises. His first impression, after he had breakfasted alone – the household, it seemed, rose late – was that Farthingdown was in such a poor state of repair, it was but a few steps from being a ruin.

It had been dark when he and Bright had arrived, and he had seen little of the house save dim-lit passages and the chamber where he had dined, which he would soon learn was the best-appointed room in the manor. His bedchamber was small and plainly furnished, and he had paid it little mind; ideally, he would not be using it for long. But having put off his sword and left it in the room, he walked out into the main hallway and received a shock.

The first things he noticed were narrow cracks in the walls, in what had once been fine stonework. Stepping to a threadbare tapestry that depicted some long-forgotten battle, he pulled it aside and saw crumbling masonry. How old the house was, he had no idea: a hundred years, perhaps more. Looking up, he discerned more cracks in the vaulted ceiling, along with dark patches of mould. There were arched passages leading away, but he decided not to explore them. Instead, he made his way to the front doors, which stood wide open. He emerged from the house into pale sunlight, walked down a set of steps into a wide courtyard, and was promptly arrested by a shout. He turned to see Tom Bright approaching. Their greeting was brief,

A RELUCTANT ASSASSIN

whereupon the sergeant wasted no time in voicing his opinion.

'Did you ever see a manor so poorly-kept, Captain?' He enquired, nodding towards the walls. 'Farthingdown, is it? *Falling-down*, the servants call it. There was some mirth about it at supper, though to my mind they're a discontented lot underneath the foolery. Their master's mad as a sack of ferrets, they say – did he strike you as such?'

Revill gave a shrug. 'He suffers from some malady, the like of which I've never seen before. You'll observe for yourself, if you see him. I'm to be shown around by the steward... a sour fellow. But aside from that, were you well bestowed?'

'Well, I'll not complain. Supper wasn't much, but I've had worse. I'm sharing a chamber with the cook and the footmen, half a dozen of us crammed together like stockfish.' He put on a wry look. 'As for the maids, none of them would give me the time of day.'

Seeing his expression, Revill almost smiled. 'I'm sorry to hear that.'

'So... am I to accompany you, on your surveying duties?' Bright enquired. 'If you don't need me, I'll be off to the stables, see the horses are content.'

Thinking it might be best to walk about Farthingdown alone with the steward, Revill was about to concur when footfalls sounded behind him. He looked round to see Ashman himself descending the steps smartly, wrapped in a heavy gown and looking ill-tempered. Without preamble, he gestured towards the gardens that lay beyond the courtyard.

'Are you ready for your tour, then?' He demanded, squinting up at Revill, who stood almost a head taller. 'And who's this rogue?'

He meant Tom Bright, whose face clouded. But when the steward's eye fell upon him, he grinned and gave a low bow, which Revill knew was done in mockery.

'This is my servant,' he said. 'He has duties, to which he was about to attend.' He paused. 'And he's no rogue, Master Ashman.'

At that, the other merely grunted. With a nod to his master, the sergeant moved off. Revill faced the steward, who seemed in haste to finish his appointed task as quickly as possible.

'In truth, I expected to walk about the house before viewing the gardens,' Revill told him. 'But since the weather is fine-'

'You'll need to see the grounds,' Ashman broke in curtly. 'The paddock and the outbuildings, stable and buttery and so forth, and lastly the house. I'm certain you'll form an opinion by mid-day, which will satisfy us both. You don't strike me as a fool, sir.'

'Satisfy us both?' Revill echoed. 'I don't follow you.'

'You don't?' The other gave a snort. 'I find that hard to compass. Surely any man with eyes in his head can see that Farthingdown is utterly unsuited to host the Queen's Progress? There's barely the capacity for a score of guests, let alone the hundreds who travel in her train - along with their horses, baggage carts and all the rest. And I won't even speak of the expense. It's preposterous... I can't imagine why any surveyor would even consider it.'

'Perhaps it's some time since one visited,' Revill remarked, after a moment. 'I'll allow that the manor looks in poor repair...'

'Poor repair?' The steward gave another contemptuous snort. 'It's as tumbledown as a Shoreditch tenement. The servants go in fear of a roof falling on their heads. Did you not look about you, when you arose this morning?'

A RELUCTANT ASSASSIN

In silence, Revill regarded him. What he had taken for the impatient manner of a scholarly man discontented with his lot, he now saw as closer to nervousness. Whereupon he recalled Lady Gisela's demeanour of the previous night, and began to form a clearer picture.

'And, if you haven't drawn your conclusions before we repair indoors for nuncheon,' Ashman went on, 'a brief survey of the house will fix them surely enough. We have few visitors here, and even fewer of noble rank. And to answer your point, no surveyor of Her Majesty's Works has never set eyes on this place, to my knowledge. As for The Queen herself, no sooner would she alight from her coach than she'd think she had been brought here in jest – or even as an insult! Do you mark me, sir?'

'And yet...' Revill drew a breath. 'Sir Abel is most taken with the notion of a royal visit...'

But he stopped himself, for the expression on the steward's face was enough. The man was right, of course: it was absurd to imagine the Queen, her courtiers and followers in all their finery descending on Farthingdown *en masse*; one look at the place would be enough. As for Sir Abel... Tom Bright's phrase came swiftly to his mind, about him being *as mad as a sack of ferrets*.

'I'll not say more, for the present,' Ashman said, with a knowing look. 'I think you understand. And I'll make your work easy for you, when you send report to your master. Likely we'll bid farewell to you soon... now, would you care to stroll? There's a lake beyond the trees, with carp. They'll probably furnish our supper.'

To that, Revill barely nodded. His feeling just then was one of mingled resignation and confusion - until he recalled the purpose of his visit, the memory of which came down upon him heavily. Somehow, he was supposed to arrange a fateful accident for Sir Abel who, for all he knew, might not even leave the house. How that might be accomplished, he hadn't the least notion.

And the hurried, round-shouldered steward was already marching off across the courtyard, drawing his thick gown about him as if it was winter already. He did not look round.

With sinking spirits, Revill followed him.

THREE

The morning was all but done, and Revill had finally taken leave of Ashman, who muttered something about papers awaiting his attention. Having now viewed almost the whole of Farthingdown, from within and without, he sat down on a stone seat, some distance from the house, and tried to collect himself. And uppermost in his mind was the fact that, if he were to carry out his sordid task, he would first need to find an excuse to prolong his visit.

The situation was troublesome, for he had little reason to stay beyond another day or so, since everything the steward had told him proved to be true. The house and outbuildings, if not the entire estate, were badly neglected, not least because he had now gathered that Sir Abel was short of money. The rents from his tenant farms brought in little, and the unpredictable nature of his condition meant than he was at times unable to manage his affairs wisely. Ashman, it seemed, did what he could out of loyalty, as his father had served the Stanburys before him. Once again Revill found himself revising his opinion of the man. As for the servants, he had found them reticent, busying themselves at their tasks and doing their best to avoid him. Ashman never spoke to them, but led the way about the manor briskly, drawing attention to a leaky section of roof with a pail set beneath it, or a door that was locked because the floor beyond it was deemed unsafe. The only conclusion to be drawn, as the steward had said, was that

Farthingdown was utterly unfit to host the Queen on her next Progress, and should be scratched from any list of destinations without delay.

He had brought out his pipe and was filling it when movement caught his eye. Looking up, he saw two figures approaching him across the untrimmed lawn, where weeds poked through the grass. Recognising one of them as Lady Gisela, he stood up at once and stowed away the pipe and tobacco.

'Master Surveyor.' The lady came up unhurriedly and stopped a short distance away. She wore a hooded cloak, her hands tucked inside a fur muff. Her companion, he saw, was a younger woman, also cloaked. Somewhat plump, round-faced and loose-lipped, she regarded him without interest, as if he were merely one of the servants.

'Madam.' Revill made his bow and assumed an expression of polite attention. 'A pleasant day, for a stroll before dinner?'

'I suppose.' Lady Gisela turned to indicate the other woman. 'Here is my daughter, Lady Charis… she was out of sorts yesternight, hence her absence from supper. Like myself, she too was somewhat surprised by your arrival.' She paused, fixing him with a steady gaze. 'I trust Ashman has satisfied your curiosity, and shown you all you needed to see?'

'He has been very accommodating,' Revill answered.

'That's well,' The mistress of Fathingdown gave a little sigh. 'In truth, I cannot help but wonder who put the notion into the heads of the Queen's Councillors, that this manor could offer her the hospitality she expects on her travels. Can you enlighten me?'

'I regret that I cannot, my lady,' Revill said, after a moment's pause. 'I'm but a servant of Her Majesty's Surveyor of Works, who-'

A RELUCTANT ASSASSIN

'Oh come, sir.' Lady Gisela cut him short. 'You're a gentleman, and nobody's lackey. Anyone can see that.'

Revill hesitated, seeking some reply. There was a look on her face which he found difficult to read. Perhaps she desired further speech with him, yet was hampered by the presence of her stolid daughter. Whereupon, the woman in question settled the matter by stifling a yawn.

'Is it not time to go to dinner, madam?' Lady Charis enquired in a bored voice. 'I've taken quite enough air, and the damp discomforts me.'

'But of course, my dear.' Her mother faced her, assuming a smile. 'I pray you, go on ahead. I will converse with our guest a while longer, then join you anon.'

'Very well, I will.' With a brief glance at him, Lady Charis turned about and walked off towards the house. And the moment she was out of earshot, Lady Gisela turned upon him with a face as hard as marble.

'So, Master... Revill, is it? What's the game, sir? You may speak freely now – indeed, I insist upon it!'

'Game, madam?' Surprised by her demeanour, Revill blinked. 'I don't understand...'

'I think you do,' the lady retorted. 'Farthingdown is a backwater, that could win prizes for dereliction. You've seen it for yourself, as I told you last night. So I desire the truth, sir, and nothing less. Who sent you here, and why? Was it to spy upon Sir Abel?'

'I assure you, it was not,' Revill said, with a shake of his head. 'You're correct that I'm nobody's lackey – and I'm no intelligencer either.'

They eyed each other: Revill uneasy while Lady Gisela, fiercely suspicious, held his gaze unflinchingly. She was still a handsome woman, he thought briefly, if aged somewhat beyond her years...

'Then what were you told, prior to coming here – I don't mean about the manor, but about my husband?' She demanded. 'I speak of the rumours that have circulated since he was last at Court, years ago though that was. They say he is mad, sir – but he is not! He suffers the indignities of his condition with stoicism – you have observed it yourself. And if he falls into fancy now and again – like this foolish desire to throw the manor open to Her Majesty, which would ruin us – he must be brought to see the hopelessness of it. Indeed, I had hoped that…'

She faltered, as if she had said more than intended. But a suspicion had arisen in Revill's mind - one that, despite her anger, he dared to voice.

'Do you mean - pardon my boldness, my lady – but are you asking me to speak privately with Sir Abel? I mean, to dissuade him from this notion of hosting the Queen?' He nodded quickly. 'For I might indeed offer some comfort in that regard. You are correct, of course: Her Majesty would not stop at Farthingdown on her Summer Progress. For myself, I'm not even certain that she intends to travel in Surrey… such matters are decided in Council, by those far above my station.'

A moment passed, in which Lady Gisela appeared to be gathering her thoughts. Finally, she looked away, towards the ancient beech trees that fringed the gardens, and her anger seemed to ebb away. 'You've small need to speak to me of decisions being made by others – or indeed, in my absence,' she murmured, as if to herself. 'But I have learned to live with them… and I love Farthingdown, with all my heart.'

She turned to meet Revill's gaze again - and in that moment, he pitied her. Like any woman of noble birth, she would have had little say in her choice of husband. And it seemed clear that her spouse was a sore trial to her - perhaps more than she deserved.

'Then, let me give what assistance I can,' he said. 'If you'll prevail upon Sir Abel to walk the gardens with me after dinner, I'll try to show him the folly of it all. Moreover,' he added on impulse, 'should he decline to walk with me, I'll persist tomorrow, and the day after, until I can be alone with him. Will that serve?'

He waited, until Lady Gisela allowed a smile to surface. 'It would serve me well...' she paused. 'So long as you remember not to take anything he may say as a personal affront. Vulgarity is but a part of his affliction. Now, shall we go in to dinner?'

***

By the early afternoon, however, Revill was having cause to regret his impulsive offer. The feeling had stolen over him during the mid-day meal, which he could hardly wait to be over. Berating himself for his weakness, brought on by some sympathy for his hostess, he was racking his brains for a solution to his predicament, which was looking uglier – if not more absurd – by the hour.

Could he really bring himself to arrange this *tragic accident* to suit Heneage, he asked himself, whatever the Vice-Chamberlain's suspicions were of Sir Abel? For if Revill had formed one clear opinion above all others, it was that the Master of Farthingdown was harmless: a trial to no-one but himself and those around him. He even liked the man a little, which was most unsoldierly for one who has been given a target to destroy. Having watched him at table again, cracking a jest with a servant and trying in vain to amuse his unsmiling daughter, Revill finally pleaded little appetite, murmured his apologies and got to his feet. But as he started to leave, he caught Lady Gisela's eye, and received a brief nod in return.

'Damn your impudence!'

Sir Abel's shout caught him unawares; he had yet to familiarise himself with these sudden outbursts. Turning, he found the man's eyes upon him, his face twitching uncontrollably. Mercifully, however, the spasm passed quite quickly.

'I pray you, Master Surveyor... ignore that.' While the others round the table eyed their platters discreetly, the knight jerked his head aside as if in pain, then lifted a hand as if to call back what he had said. 'My wife has suggested that you and I walk together - I'll be outside in an hour. Are you content?'

'I am, sir,' Revill replied. And having made a hasty obeisance, he went.

An hour later, the Master of Farthingdown emerged from the doors of the manor in a heavy outdoor gown, and found Revill waiting. With a cheery smile, his host gestured him to come to his side as if they were old friends.

'Have you seen the lake?' He asked, without preamble. And before Revill could answer: 'It's deep as a chasm in the centre. A boy drowned in it once... groom's son. Couldn't swim, poor fellow.'

'Master Ashman showed it to me, sir,' Revill answered, ashamed of a thought that sprang to his mind: here was one means of staging an accident. 'It's a most beautiful vista - as indeed, is all your land.' For that much was true: despite its condition, the old manor's setting was as pleasant and tranquil as any he had seen.

'Damn the man!'

The words flew from Sir Abel's mouth; Revill lowered his gaze and ignored them. In silence the two of them began to walk from courtyard to garden, where an aged gardener was now raking fallen leaves, and thence through the trees into a meadow that sloped down towards the lake.

A RELUCTANT ASSASSIN

His host was humming an air to himself, that Revill failed to recognise. Finally, the man turned and asked him what he now thought of Farthingdown.

'As I said, sir,' Revill replied, 'it's as fair a place as I've ever set eyes on-'

'No - I mean as a place to host Her Royal Majesty, when she comes to Surrey. Would she not delight in these surroundings? It would gladden my heart to see it!'

Revill stiffened: the matter was broached before he had fully marshalled his arguments. He drew a breath, and faced it.

'Sir Abel... if you'll allow, I must speak plainly with you,' he began. 'My commission, as you know, was to make inspection of your house and grounds, to ascertain their suitability to host the Queen's train - perhaps for some days, or even longer. It's... in truth, it would be a vast undertaking for any landowner, providing bed and board for so many people. Not to mention feeding and stabling for their horses, entertainment and-'

'What – do you think I cannot afford to do it?'

The other stopped walking and turned a sharp eye upon Revill. 'You deem me a pauper?'

'No, sir... but hear me, if you will. The Queen's Courtiers, and all those close to her, would expect the highest standards of hospitality from you – hunting and feasting, dancing and the like. For instance, you may recall the Princely Pleasures that the Earl of Leicester staged for her at Kenilworth, fourteen years ago. I'm speaking of an enormous outlay-'

'By God, you *do* think me a pauper – and a fool to boot!'

Sir Abel cut him off, wearing a look of mingled anger and consternation. 'Is that what you've been told, sir?' He continued, his agitation growing as he spoke. 'For I well know there are men on the Council who despise me... who have mocked me, and spread cruel rumours – lies, all of it!'

The man's face began to twitch, as he struggled to master himself. Revill was on the point of asking him if they should return to the house, but instead he waited until the spasm had passed. At last, his host appeared to recover, and fixed him with a frown.

'Perhaps I should have known,' he said, somewhat breathlessly. 'I can hardly lay blame upon you, who have only your instructions. You've seen the condition of some of the walls, and the roof, and drawn your conclusions – but listen to me. Such things can be remedied by next summer – in truth, I've engaged tilers from Weybridge to make repairs to the roof already. They were to start after Christmas, but I'll order them to come tomorrow. I can hire masons too, and carpenters. Rooms that are disused may be opened up... do you see?'

'I do, sir... indeed, I applaud your vision,' Revill said. 'It's merely that-'

'The costs, you mean?' Sir Abel waved a hand as if to dismiss the question. 'Let me set your mind at rest there. I'm due certain monies that will change matters hugely – any day, in fact. The lawyers are busy as we speak. Likely your master is unaware of my pending suit, that will enlarge Farthingdown by many acres. Has no-one told you of my dispute with a man named John Cowley?'

'They have not, sir,' Revill replied. Upon which, his host grew animated again.

'A neighbour, whose land borders mine to the south. A grasping, mendacious farmer who would swear on the Bible that day is night...' he breathed in heavily, and gave a quick shake of his head. 'And yet, my late father and his late father were firm friends – to cap it all, when they were boys a-swimming in the Wey once, my father as good as saved Samuel Cowley's life! Now his son and I are enemies - and a bitter pill to swallow, is that. It pains Lady Gisela as it does me, to think of what's been done…' he let out a sigh. 'In short, there was a clause in old Cowley's will, leaving a goodly portion of his pasture to me, in reward for my father's brave action. But now, by God…'

Sir Abel broke off, wincing as the very thought pained him. He shuddered, as if at a sudden chill, then faced Revill again.

'The nub of the matter is Cowley disputes it. He claims his father changed the terms of his will before he died – and that the old one is lost. Lies, sir – brazen lies, borne of the man's greed and ingratitude! But he will pay – as I've said, my lawyers will make him!'

He fell silent, and Revill had no words of reply. His first thought was that the man was clutching at straws. And yet, even if it were true, he told himself – even if the repairs his host had mentioned were done - the fact still remained that Farthingdown was too small and too humble a destination for the Queen. Elizabeth was accustomed to staying at the castles and great houses of the richest landowners, who vied to outdo one another with lavish hospitality in hopes of preferment at Court. Sir Abel, despite his ancestry, was not one of them… and somehow, he must be made to see it.

'I hear you, sir,' he said finally. 'And it's my earnest wish that your suit progresses to your satisfaction. Yet, when all's been said, I'm compelled to lay forth the difficulties that still confront you. In short, when I return to London I must inform Master Blagrave of your position, without favour. That is, my report will…'

But he stopped himself, for Sir Abel wasn't listening. After gazing into the distance for a while he turned, his face brightening.

'And of course, there's the matter of the marriage!' He exclaimed. 'I should have spoken of that, too.' And when Revill raised his brows, he added: 'My daughter Lady Charis is to be married in the spring, to a man of substance. The settlement is yet to be agreed, of course, but...' He waved a hand, as if that clinched the matter – and Revill's heart sank.

Sir Abel Stanbury, he saw, lived in a world of dreams and desires, bound together with nothing but hope. His conversation that morning with Lady Gisela had forced him to view her husband's pronouncements with scepticism, if not downright disbelief. As for their daughter's betrothal to *a man of substance...* it was of course possible, but somehow, he found it hard to imagine. And besides, was it not the father of the bride who was expected to provide the dowry?

He lowered his gaze. And when his host began to stroll again, pointing out the beauty of his woodlands in their autumn glory, he could do nothing but walk beside him and make polite reply from time to time.

His promise to Lady Gisela, to convince her husband that his plans amounted to mere fancies, remained unfulfilled.

***

That evening, after supper, he sought out Tom Bright and found him in the stables gossiping with other men. On his master's entrance, the sergeant left their company and came forward.

'I saw you walking earlier, Captain,' he murmured, as they both stepped outside. 'After what happened with the

A RELUCTANT ASSASSIN

steward today, I thought it best to keep out of sight. Have you found out what you needed?'

'You might say so,' Revill answered. He was irritable and low in spirits, and felt almost inclined to unburden himself. Instead, he asked Bright how he'd passed the time.

'Well, I've been doing just what you said,' was his reply. 'Taking a holiday.' He paused. 'How much longer do you think it'll last?'

Revill merely shrugged.

'You're not done, then? I mean, with this Court business?' He regarded his old captain with a shrewd look, which Revill knew well enough. Drawing a breath, he shook his head.

'If you're finding yourself at a loose end, I'd understand if you wanted to get back to London. I'll pay your wage.'

'Oh, indeed?' Bright narrowed his eyes. 'You mean, you'd prefer to be left alone here?'

'Well... perhaps I would.'

He glanced about the cobbled yard, with its flickering torches. From within the stable, the voices and occasional laughter of Farthingdown men could be heard.

'Your pardon, Captain,' the sergeant said after a moment, 'but I'm troubled – on your account, that is. You were glum enough on the ride down here, and now you're even glummer. Will you not speak plain to me, like you used to?'

Their eyes met - and Revill stiffened: on a sudden, it was as if the past year had fallen away. In the lurid torchlight where they stood, he could almost see the battlefield: the cannon-smoke billowing about him, the distant flames, the pitiful cries of the wounded... he saw Bright in shirt-sleeves, a filthy rag tied about his head, frantically wedging the gun-trail while Klaas, the young

Zeelander, rammed wads of oakum down the barrel of the culverin. The other Dutchman, Cornelius, was yelling something he couldn't understand - and then came the deafening blast, that had stopped his heart...

With an effort he brought himself to his senses, drawing in a deep gout of night air. In the stable-yard Bright was before him, still wearing a questioning look.

'I can't, Tom,' he said at last. 'Not just now.'

'Very well...' the sergeant gave a sigh. 'I'll wander over to the kitchen, beg a mug of ale.' He hesitated, then: 'As for finding myself at a loose end, that isn't likely. I might have spoken too soon, concerning the Farthingdown wenches... there's one, anyway.'

He put on a knowing look, whereupon they parted.

As night settled over the manor, Revill took a last stroll about the gardens. But by the time he returned to the house, his thoughts had strayed from present matters to settle on Jenna, and what she would think of his mission. Whereupon he reminded himself of why he was here, and forced himself to picture his sweet-natured sister, happy in her newly wedded state... of course, he told himself harshly, to refuse Heneage's instruction would be impossible.

On a sudden, he found himself cursing the Queen's elegant, soft-spoken Vice-Chamberlain from the very depths of his heart. But it didn't help much.

FOUR

The next day, with a mist lying over Farthingdown, Revill rose early, skipped breakfast and went directly to the stables. He wore his soldier's coat over his doublet, and his tawny riding gloves; it had not occurred to him to dress in any special way for his sojourn into Surrey. Finding no-one about, he took Malachi from the stall, saddled him and led him out into the grey morning. He was restless, having barely slept, and keen to put some distance between himself and the manor. Within minutes he had ridden out of the gates and onto a narrow lane which led southwards, where the ground rose slightly. Soon he was passing through pastures, with the forms of grazing sheep dimly visible in the mist. Slowing the horse to a walk, he at last allowed himself to think.

But of course, nothing had changed. Nor would it, until he either found a way of contriving this tragic mishap for Sir Abel, the thought of which dismayed him, or found some means to avoid it. Wild notions had already occurred to him: to confess everything to his host and Lady Gisela, and let them take whatever action they chose; to ride to Katherine in Barnstaple, two hundred miles away, and warn her and her husband of the danger they were in; or even to confront Heneage – tell him Sir Abel was a sick man, and no danger to anyone. Though he suspected the last of those would result in his being arrested. Then again, having warned his sister, he could even take ship from the very town where she lived, and return to active service in Flanders...

With a sudden oath, he brought Malachi to a halt, railing at his own folly. The old warhorse snorted, causing Revill to bend low and calm him. *What a dolt you are*, he told himself. *Would you really go back to that blood-soaked land? To return to slaughtering Spaniards - to laying siege against towns full of innocent Dutchmen and women, let alone children...*

Sitting forlornly on his horse in the middle of the lane, he sagged.

Finally, he dismounted, led Malachi to the side of the road and wound the reins about a sapling. Then he forced his way through a hedge, walked through wet grass and found an old tree stump on which to sit. And there he stayed, as the mist slowly lifted and weak sunlight began to filter through the haze, while distant birdsong lulled him into a doze. I've slept in worse places, he thought vaguely - until a shout woke him, bringing him bolt upright.

The shout, challenging in tone, came from no more than a dozen yards away. As he sprang to his feet his soldier's instinct took over, making him reach swiftly for his poniard; his sword he had left at the manor. But as he did so, he was startled to see a large black-and-white dog bounding towards him. There was no threat, however: the dog slowed down, its tongue hanging out, and stopped before him.

'You there! What's your business?'

He looked up to see a tall figure striding forward, wearing a shepherd's cape. Relaxing slightly, he sheathed the poniard and waited. The figure soon revealed himself to be a bony, hatchet-faced man with a heavy beard, wearing a most unfriendly expression.

A RELUCTANT ASSASSIN

'My business?' Revill spread his hands. 'I have none. Just resting a little.' To diffuse the situation, he bent down and greeted the dog, ruffling its shaggy coat. Still suspicious, the tall man looked him over.

'This is my pasture,' he said, after a moment. 'Strangers can frighten the sheep... and it strikes me as an odd place to take a rest.'

'I'm a guest of your neighbour, at Farthingdown,' Revill told him. 'And I mean no harm to you or your sheep.'

But the other tensed at once. 'At Stanbury's?' His face hardened. 'By the Christ, I should have guessed!'

It was then that Revill knew the man's identity. He had to be the John Cowley that Sir Abel had railed against: his opponent in the lawsuit on which he had pinned his hopes.

'Sir Abel and Lady Gisela are indeed my hosts,' he replied. 'And since I'm unwelcome here, I'll take my leave...'

But as he was about to turn, the other took a step forward. 'One moment,' he said. 'Did you break my hedge to get in here?'

'I merely parted it,' Revill said, growing weary of the discourse. 'I'm from a farming family myself, and know better than-'

'Who are you, then?' The other snapped. 'Did Stanbury ask you to poke around? It wouldn't surprise me.'

'Are you Master Cowley?' Revill countered, raising his eyebrows. 'Somehow, that doesn't surprise me, either.'

'And what do you mean by that, pray?'

'Let's say I've heard your name spoken, along with a few hints as to your nature.'

'From Stanbury, you mean?' Cowley turned away and spat heavily on to the grass. 'Well, you're a fool if you believe a word he says. Anyone hereabouts can tell you that!'

Revill let out a sigh. 'I'll decide for myself who to believe. And as for naming me a fool...' he met the other man's eye. 'You don't know me. If you did, you'd have thought better.'

A moment passed, before Master Cowley seemed to reconsider. Finally, he muttered something under his breath, and took a step back.

'I'll ask your pardon for it,' he said. 'Then, you don't know me either. Likely you've heard badly of me from Stanbury... talk of wills and lawyers, no doubt. But there's two sides to any case, wouldn't you say?'

Revill said nothing, but glanced down at the dog which appeared to have been watching their exchange with interest. Finally, it wandered back to its master, sniffing at the ground.

'You didn't tell me your name,' Cowley said then.

'That's true,' Revill said. Again, he turned to go, but again, the other man stayed him.

'See now, I know I...' he seemed to be fumbling for the words. 'This business with Stanbury, it's made me mad. There are times I can't see straight...' he rubbed his beard, then: 'Are you a friend of his?'

'In a way,' Revill answered. He was thinking that, for a landowner, Cowley dressed poorly. Anyone might have taken him for a shepherd, rather than the owner of the flock and the land upon which it grazed.

'Then, by heaven, I wish I could prevail upon you to make the man see sense!' He blurted, with sudden vehemence. 'Others have tried - even his wife, from what I hear. But he's deaf to all reason – and addle-headed. You must know that.'

A RELUCTANT ASSASSIN

'I'll allow Sir Abel has his eccentricities. But I'd not call him mad,' was Revill's reply.

'You wouldn't?' Cowley returned. 'Then you don't know the half of it, my friend. He means to ruin me – see me lose my farm, and everything on it! Me, with a wife and six young ones to feed, and debts enough to drive a man to his grave! How's that for eccentricity?' Whereupon he swore an oath and banged a fist angrily against his side. The dog looked at him anxiously.

'You have my sympathies, but it's none of my affair,' Revill said, berating himself for ever trespassing on to the man's land. And this time, when he turned to take his leave, he would not be stayed. Without looking back he walked to the hedge, pushed his way through again and stepped into the lane, where Malachi lifted his head at once.

'What in God's name are you and I doing here?' He murmured, as he tugged the reins free.

The horse gave him a sidelong look.

***

That afternoon a visitor arrived at Farthingdown, taking Revill by surprise. After his morning ride in the quiet Surrey lanes, which had cleared his head a little, he took a noon meal with the family before retiring to his chamber to catch a little sleep. He was awoken by loud voices from downstairs, along with squeals of laughter. Rousing himself, he straightened his appearance and ventured down to the main entrance hall. There he found Sir Abel and Lady Gisela, along with their daughter, in conversation with a gentleman in riding clothes. And from the behaviour of Lady Charis, he guessed that the newcomer was here on her behalf: the young woman, flushed and smiling, appeared most glad to see him.

'Master Surveyor!' Sir Abel, somewhat animated, turned to greet him. 'I present Richard Norris - the suitor I spoke of earlier.' He gestured Revill forward, then faced Norris again. 'Here's the man who will open the door for us, sir,' he announced. 'To hosting the Queen, no less!'

Norris, a broad-faced man with a russet beard, eyed Revill with interest. But as they exchanged a brief greeting, a warning bell sounded in his head, along with the suspicion that he had seen this person before. Though where that might be, he could not recall. The other gave no sign of recognising him in turn.

'Your servant, sir,' the visitor murmured, with a faint smile. 'You must tell me more of this... door-opening power which you possess.'

Revill met his eye, but kept expression from his face; the smile, he now thought, appeared sardonic. With a brief nod, he mentioned his commission from the Queen's Surveyor of Works. As he did so he caught Lady Gisela's eye - and read a warning. *Tread with care*, the lady seemed to be saying. Or more likely, perhaps she was reminding him that his promise to her, given somewhat rashly, was still to be kept.

But the moment of tension was broken by Lady Charis, who was eager almost to the point of breaking into a sweat. Only now did Revill notice that she was dressed in what must be her finest – jewels and a heavily-embroidered gown of red, blue and gold, cut so low it was almost indecent. He had seen trulls dress less enticingly.

'You were expected yesternight, sir!' She gushed, ignoring Revill pointedly and wagging a finger at Norris. 'Yet we may forgive your tardiness... may we not, madam?' She turned to her mother, who barely nodded.

'Come into the marigold room, Master Norris, and take wine and cakes,' she said smoothly. 'How was your ride?'

A RELUCTANT ASSASSIN

And with that, she indicated a doorway which led to one of the more presentable rooms of Farthingdown. As the party began to move, Revill took a discreet pace away, having no desire to intrude. Whereupon to his surprise, Norris contrived to step close to him, and bent his head briefly.

'The brewhouse, an hour after supper,' he said quietly. 'Don't disappoint me.'

Then he was away, giving his full attention to the Lady Charis.

Taken aback, Revill, watched the two of them in silence – whereupon another thing struck him: while the Stanbury daughter was gazing up at Norris in something akin to rapture, the other's feelings fell far short of such sentiment. In short, he guessed, the man cared not a jot for her, but was acting a part: one that appeared to fool everyone, apart from him.

***

That night, which was clear and cold with a rising breeze, Revill left the manor and walked round by the stables towards the little stone brewhouse that stood by itself. The place was dark, lit faintly by a three-quarter moon, and when he tried the door, he found it locked. Glancing about, he saw no-one, and wondered how long he should wait. Norris's tone, when he had spoken privately to him earlier, had been urgent. Throughout supper, however, the man had ignored him, which only added to the mystery. Since then, he had trawled his memory for memories as to where he might have encountered him, to no avail.

He drew in a breath of chilly air; if Norris did not appear soon, he decided, he would seek out Tom Bright, if only for his company. At which moment, there came a footfall from close by and a shape loomed out of the dark.

'I'll be brief with you, Revill,' Norris said at once. 'You've been here – what, three days? And nothing done. I speak of your commission... would you care to give an explanation?'

'To you?' Revill said, collecting himself. 'I wasn't aware I owed you any such thing - sir.'

'See now, I'm not here to waste time,' the other said harshly. He had moved closer, his face just visible in the moonlight. 'I know what Heneage's orders are. Yet I find you idling, seemingly content to enjoy Sir Abel's hospitality, such as it is. Even your servant, from what I've heard, treats the place as his own. How's that, pray?'

In the silence that followed Revill eyed the man, making a rapid assessment of his capabilities. He wore a sword, and looked as if he knew how to use it. But Revill was wearing his too, this night – merely as a precaution, he had told himself.

'So then, you've come to check on my progress,' he said finally. 'I'd been led to believe you were a family friend – a suitor to Lady Charis. An odd coincidence, isn't it?'

At that, he saw the other stiffen. For a moment they eyed each other, then:

'I didn't think I'd need to remind you of your position, Revill,' Norris said in a voice of menace. 'But you know what penalty you face if you fail to-'

'What makes you think I'll fail?' Revill broke in. 'Perhaps it's I who need to remind you, that someone in my position must first win the trust of the family. Otherwise, had the matter been despatched within a day or two, Lady Gisela and her daughter – not to mention their steward - might look upon me somewhat suspiciously, wouldn't you say so?'

A RELUCTANT ASSASSIN

But Norris was unmoved. 'To my mind, that has the whiff of an excuse about it,' he retorted. 'What does it matter to you what they all think? You carry out your task, and then leave before they have time to get over the shock. Unless…' On a sudden, he let out a snort of laughter. 'By God, you aren't smitten with her, are you? That old harpy? But then, you wouldn't be the first. She wears well for her age, I suppose.'

Taut as a wand, Revill drew a breath. 'I'm no more smitten with Lady Stanbury than you are with her daughter,' he answered. 'Or did you think nobody has noticed?'

But to that, the other's response was swift: in the gloom, Revill saw his hand fly to his sword-hilt. Dropping his own hand, he took a short step back.

'Have a care, Norris,' he said gently. 'You wouldn't want to draw blade against me.'

'No – *you* have a care,' Norris snapped. 'My affairs are naught to you – and nor will I tarry here for long. All you need know is that if Sir Abel is still alive by the time I leave, I go straight to Heneage. Whatever befalls you after that is no-one's fault but your own.' He gave a sniff of contempt. 'Or should I say, whatever befalls your Papist sister!'

For a second, Revill fought to stay his temper - but of course, it was hopeless. His hand left his sword-hilt, and shot out to grasp Norris by the throat. The man grunted and seized his wrist – and at once the two were locked in a tussle, falling against the rough wall of the brewhouse, their breath clouding in the air. But as Norris lurched aside, his hand darted behind his back – and Revill felt the icy coldness of the poniard pressed to his neck.

It was his assailant's mistake.

With a brief sigh, he let go of Norris's throat, snatched the hand holding the poniard and bent it aside with force. The result was a cry of pain, followed by the clatter of the weapon falling to the ground. But even as it fell, Revill's own poniard was out of its sheath, its point jabbed under the man's chin. With barely a shove, the skin would break.

'Be still,' he muttered. 'Or I'll pin your tongue to your palate.'

Norris went rigid, breathing fast while hisses of pain escaped his lips.

'Now fall to your knees.'

With a gasp of mingled anger and hurt, Norris did as he was ordered, taking his sprained wrist in his other hand and working it. Swiftly, Revill switched his poniard to his left hand, drew his sword and put its point to the man's chest.

'Now I think you and I should have a proper talk,' he said.

He sheathed the poniard, while the other looked balefully up at him.

'Firstly, what's Heneage to you?' Revill demanded. 'Are you one of his lackeys?'

'To the devil with you!' Norris blurted. 'When he learns of this you're finished, you-'

Revill jerked the sword, almost hard enough to pierce the man's doublet.

'I suspect he hasn't told you much – about me, I mean,' he said. 'I'm the sort who would despatch you with ease, tie your corpse to my horse's saddle and haul you off up the lane, leave you under a hedge somewhere. In the morning they'd find you stripped and robbed, and raise the hue and cry for priggers. I hear they're often active on Weybridge Heath, and hereabouts. I, of course, would be most eager to join in the hunt for the murderers.'

A RELUCTANT ASSASSIN

'Good Christ...' suddenly Norris gave a shiver; the night was indeed cold, and he wasn't dressed for it. 'You wouldn't - Heneage would know, and you'd be a fugitive yourself!'

Gazing down at him, Revill was about to make reply - when on a sudden, recognition dawned: at last, he knew where he had seen this man.

'Why - you're not Norris,' he exclaimed. 'You're Lewis Turnbull... I saw you at Flushing!'

The other caught his breath.

'You served Sir Philip Sidney, God rest him. Though you left soon after he fell, did you not?' Feeling his irritation rise, Revill leaned forward. 'So - you turned intelligencer, did you? Scratching about in the dirt, once Heneage found a use for you. Now you're playing that young woman for a fool, pretending affection for her – why's that?'

But Norris – or rather, Lewis Turnbull, as he was now revealed to be – merely met his gaze. His expression was bleak, and Revill knew that look. He had seen it on the faces of prisoners, resigned to their fate.

'Well then,' he said with a sigh. 'So, we know each other. What say we make a bargain? My secret stays with me, and yours stays with you. Will you trade?'

'No... not yet.' Keeping his sword pressed to the man's breastbone, Revill shook his head. 'First, I want some answers. Such as why, in God's name, is Heneage so eager to have Sir Abel put to death? He's an innocent – about as dangerous as a rabbit.'

'By heaven, what does it matter?' Turnbull demanded, somewhat bitterly. 'You know he'd not be the first innocent man to die, in these times - nor the last. Why can't you just carry out your orders, and be done with it?'

'I'll say to you what I said to Heneage,' Revill answered. 'I'm a soldier – not an assassin.'

'Oh indeed?' Suddenly, the man's anger quickened. Cold and sore where he knelt, still massaging his wrist, he grimaced. 'And were you just a soldier at Axel, when men were slaughtered – unarmed, and pleading for their lives? You're a butcher, sir!'

Revill went rigid, feeling the colour drain from his face. For a moment their eyes met... until abruptly, he lowered his sword. A look of alarm crossed Turnbull's features, followed by one of surprise when, without warning, he found himself seized by the collar and yanked to his feet.

'Now talk,' Revill said, in a tone that brooked no refusal. 'And when you're done, I'll think on the bargain you offered. Are you willing, or not?'

Startled, the other drew back. He glanced about, then: 'I suppose you might consider the son,' he said, with some weariness. 'Hugh Stanbury...' he frowned. 'What, did you not know the Stanburys have a son?'

Slowly, Revill shook his head.

'You should,' the other said. 'He's one of your kind - a wounded bear, mad for the fight. But he's on a rope, and Heneage holds the other end...' he paused. 'You'll want to know more, of course – but I'll be damned if I'll tell it. Now I'm walking away, and you can do as you please!'

With a sudden movement Lewis Turnbull, minor intelligencer for the Crown, turned aside and stumbled off into the gloom, still clutching his injured wrist. And all Revill could do was watch him go... until his gaze fell to the ground, where the man's poniard still lay.

Absently he stooped to pick it up, then decided to leave it where it was.

FIVE

Just before dawn Revill woke with a jolt, a single word echoing in his head: *Mercy!* And in a moment, he had thrown aside the coverlet and stumbled to his feet, standing in the cold chamber in his nightshirt.

Axel... the memory, stark and terrible, had been stirred up by Turnbull - though in truth, he dreamed of it often enough. The town on the Scheldt estuary, occupied by the Spanish, and now a target for the eighteen-year-old Prince Maurice in his first battle. They had laid siege, the force of mixed Dutchmen and English, sweating in the summer heat... he recalled the brave advance party under Colonel Pyrom, swimming the moat and scaling the walls. Soon the gates were opened, and in they surged: first the Dutch, savage in their assault on the hated occupiers, then the English under dashing Sir Philip Sidney, who would lose his life a few months later at Zutphen. Finally, Willoughby's troops had entered the town – not only to witness the slaughter, but to join in it. And Revill...

Revill wasn't even supposed to be there. His men had been hauling their cannon upriver, for reasons he barely remembered, when they had found themselves ordered to leave the guns and join the assault. When they came into Axel it was a scene of carnage, the Spanish garrison sorely outnumbered... though they had fought gallantly, their fate was sealed. Finding himself in a swordfight with a desperate, exhausted Spanish officer, he had overpowered the man, forcing him to drop his weapon – and then the cry, in English: *Mercy! Señor... for the love of God... have mercy...*

But to his shame, Revill had shown none. And this time, instead of forcing the memory away, he faced it. There in the dusty street, beset by cries of the wounded and dying, breathless with battle-fever, he had let his soldier's instinct rule him, and dealt the death blow. Then he had watched the man expire, choking on his own blood.

Now, dimly aware of the first fingers of dawn showing at the window, he slumped down on the bed and voiced the question he had asked himself, many times.

When will I be free of this?

But as always, there was no answer – and now he was under orders, to put to death a man who had done nothing to deserve it. Shivering, he crawled under the coverlet and tried to return to sleep, without success.

***

By mid-morning he was out in the courtyard. He had not seen Tom Bright and was about to look for him, when his attention was caught by noises from somewhere above his head, seemingly from the east wing of the manor. With little else to do but brood, he walked round the corner to find a long ladder set against a wall. Then he remembered Sir Abel's words, about repairs to the roof. Looking up, he saw two men at work high above, sitting astride the ridge, the clatter of their tools ringing in the crisp morning air. For a while he watched them, until a familiar greeting made him turn. And here was the Master of Farthingdown himself, apparently in good spirits.

'As you see, I'm a man of my word, Master Surveyor!' Sir Abel beamed. 'Tilers from Weybridge... the best, I'm assured. You may inspect their work yourself when it's done.'

A RELUCTANT ASSASSIN

But after making polite greeting, Revill was silent; he could not bring himself to lie, to voice approval at this development. He merely accompanied his host as he walked about, noting a few broken tiles which had apparently been dislodged already. There was a wheelbarrow nearby full of new tiles, and beside it rolled sheets of tarred sailcloth, which he assumed were to cover any gaps in the roof against the rain.

'God's thunder!'

Startled, he turned to see Sir Abel, his face twisted in one of his spasms; his mind elsewhere, he had almost forgotten the man's affliction. He waited for the attack to pass.

'Christ's blood!'

Sir Abel jerked as if struck, then shook himself like a dog. Unable to help him Revill looked about, just as someone else rounded the corner of the house: Ashman the steward, with whom he had barely spoken since their tour. At sight of them the man came forward... whereupon there was a sudden cry of alarm, that startled Revill anew. This one, however, came from above his head – and as his gaze flew upward, he saw the danger.

'Get back!'

Without a second thought, Revill acted. From the corner of his eye, he saw the tiles sliding off the roof – two or three of them, about to hurtle downwards, directly above Sir Abel where he stood. Leaping forward, he seized the man with both arms and threw him aside, the two of them landing in a heap on the roof-cloths. At the same instant the tiles crashed to the ground, breaking into smithereens. The noise was followed by cries from above, and another from Ashman who was only yards away. But Revill breathed a sigh of relief and got to his knees.

'Are you hurt, sir?' He peered down at Sir Abel, who was lying motionless... until thankfully, he too let out a breath and lifted his head.

'Hurt... am I hurt?' He met Revill's anxious look. 'I think not... but what the devil...?'

Stiffly, Revill stood up and reached down to take him by the arm. Ashman came up, muttering under his breath, and took the other arm. Between them they raised Sir Abel to his feet, where he stood in something of a daze. His face twitching, he stared about, saw the smashed tiles and at last turned to his steward.

'God in heaven, Ashman,' he murmured. 'I think our guest has just saved my life.'

There was a moment, as the three of them stared at each other. Finally, as one, they looked upwards to the men responsible for the accident – which, of course, it was. With an odd mixture of feelings, Revill watched as one of them slid hurriedly to the ladder's head on his rump, then clambered down. Once on the ground, the man dropped to one knee before the Master of Farthingdown and dashed off his cap.

'Your pardon, sir,' he breathed, with head bowed. 'I pray you, forgive me... I tried to warn you – by the Christ, I swear I did-'

'Enough, for pity's sake!'

In embarrassment, Sir Abel silenced him. 'Get up, fellow,' he added. 'I'm not an archbishop.' He turned to Revill. 'But if I were, likely this man would be rewarded better than I can do...' Letting out a sigh, he put out a hand, and Revill took it.

'Let's not fall to fancy, sir,' he said. 'I suspect you'd have suffered cuts and bruises had you been struck, but little more. To say I saved your life seems... well, excessive.'

A RELUCTANT ASSASSIN

'Even so, you deserve thanks for your prompt action.'

He looked round, to see Ashman gazing at him.

'It was a courageous act,' the steward said. 'But as for you, Fordham...' with a severe look he turned upon the hapless workman, who had risen to stand before them, cap in hand. 'I never saw such carelessness... you're dismissed. Get you gone!'

The man gulped, crushing his cap. 'Save you, Master Ashman,' he began, 'I swear I-'

'You will swear nothing,' the steward snapped. 'And as for your-'

'Ashman, that's quite enough.'

It was Sir Abel, waving a hand, as was his habit, as if he could waft the whole business away. 'I will not have the man dismissed,' he went on. 'I need the work done, and it was but a mishap.' He let out a breath and faced the tiler. 'Return to your task, fellow. Just be sure you watch who's walking below... I'm counting on you.'

Whereupon, with an enormous sigh of relief, Master Fordham bowed, muttered his thanks and went back to his ladder.

Revill watched him climb. He might not truly have saved Sir Abel's life, and yet... he turned to see Ashman walking off, head bowed. But Sir Abel was eying him with a broad smile.

'We'll talk further over our dinner,' he said.

***

They were five at table: Sir Abel and Lady Gisela, Lady Charis seated beside Turnbull, as Revill now knew him, and Revill himself. Ashman was called elsewhere, it seemed. Naturally enough, the talk turned to the morning's mishap, and the Master of Farthingdown's fortunate escape.

'Now I think upon it, the affair must have had a comic aspect to it,' Sir Abel said, waving his wine-cup. 'Knockabout stuff, fit for the playhouse – eh, Master Surveyor?'

Revill gave a dismissive smile and took up his own cup. He was aware of Turnbull eying him across the table, but avoided the man's gaze. He had a fair notion of what Lady Charis's shady suitor might think about his action of that morning.

'Comical or not, we are grateful to you, sir,' Lady Gisela said, with a faint smile. 'Your intervention was timely and brave... worthy of the soldier you were.'

Embarrassed, Revill sought to change the subject, whereupon Turnbull spoke up. 'I will add my contribution to the praise and plaudits, sir.' With a gesture that Revill knew was one of mockery, he lifted his cup. 'I salute your courage, and drink to your good health.'

'Christ's passion!'

Sir Abel's sudden outburst startled the man, who seemed less accustomed to his future father-in-law's ways than the family. Even Revill barely reacted, as his host fell to his usual pattern of twitching followed by recovery. Instead, he eyed Turnbull, acknowledging his toast.

'I thank you – sir. But I fear you over-egg the pudding. Any man would have acted as I did - as I'm certain you would put Sir Abel or any of his family before your own safety.'

The other met his gaze, and a hostile look flitted across his features. Whereupon his bride-to-be, who had not ceased eating throughout the exchange, lifted her head suddenly.

'Master Norris seldom dispenses praise to any man, sir,' she said to Revill, her large eyes peering into his. 'You have earned even his respect.'

A RELUCTANT ASSASSIN

Eager to move away from this discourse, on a sudden Revill found a memory from his confrontation with her paramour coming to mind. For better or worse, he decided to voice it.

'I hear you have a son, Sir Abel,' he said, turning to face him. 'Hugh Stanbury, is it not? I may have heard the name... is he at Court?'

The result, to his surprise, was a sudden and complete silence.

'Have I spoken amiss?' He asked, after a pause. He looked round the table, but no-one met his gaze. Turnbull began eating, as did Lady Charis, while Sir Abel was looking away, seemingly on the verge of a spasm. Finally, Lady Gisela dabbed at her mouth with a napkin and spoke up.

'Our son is in the Queen's service overseas, Master Revill. On matters of a diplomatic nature, that we are not privy to.'

'Then, I understand,' Revill replied. 'I pray you, excuse my forwardness.'

The lady gave a nod and took up her spoon, signalling the end of the matter. Revill did the same, but his mind was busy: something was amiss, and his curiosity was aroused. He waited until conversation of an everyday sort gradually arose again, prompted by Lady Gisela's small-talk. Whereupon he was relieved to leave the table and walk outside, heading for the gardens as had almost become his habit.

Having a need to seek out Tom Bright, he made his way to the stables, but failed to find him. After seeing that Malachi was well-fed and contented, he asked a stable-lad if he had seen the sergeant, only to receive a shake of the head.

'No sign of him all day, sir,' was his reply. But a sly look appeared, that aroused Revill's suspicions.

'Yet, I'm guessing you have a notion where he might be?' He raised an eyebrow. The boy hesitated, whereupon he reached for his purse, opened it and found a penny. 'Take this, in thanks for caring for my horse. You follow?'

'I do, sir - and I thank you kindly.' The lad took the coin and touched his cap, then: 'I couldn't swear to it, master, but there's a little hut beyond the paddock. It used to be the falconer's when we had one. Almost a ruin now, but... well, some folk find a use for it.'

'Do they, now,' Revill replied.

'They do, sir... but like I say, I couldn't swear to it.'

He was still wearing his sly look as Revill turned and left him.

A short while later, relieved to be putting a distance between himself and the manor again, he was skirting the paddock behind the stables, where a few mounts had been put out to graze. He soon found the hut, and was unsurprised to see it in poor repair, the thatch sagging and green with moss. He approached it somewhat warily, preparing to make a noise that would warn Bright of his approach, if he was inside. It would not be the first time he had been obliged to interrupt his rutting sergeant at his pleasures, he thought wryly... then, barely two yards from the closed door of the hut, he halted.

He had heard a sound from within – but it sounded like an oath, or even a cry of rage. He hesitated only briefly, then stepped forward and opened the door... to stop in surprise.

Seated on an upturned barrel, his doublet unbuttoned and a stoneware flagon in his hand, was Ashman the steward.

A RELUCTANT ASSASSIN

'Good Christ...' the man gave a start, then with something like a moan he sagged, to gaze down at the earth floor. 'You, of all people... what do you want?'

'Merely poking about, as is my habit,' Revill answered. He glanced around and saw another flagon in a corner. Even from the doorway Ashman's breath stank of strong drink; indeed, the whole hut stank. Was this a regular haunt of his, he wondered – a place to escape from the cares of his office?

'Well, since there's naught to see,' the steward retorted in a surly tone, 'I'll ask you to take yourself off. Go and inspect something else. Inspect your own arse, for all I care.'

For a moment Revill eyed him. He had seen men in his condition more times than he cared to recall, drowning their tribulations in drink. But he had not expected such from Sir Abel's steward. On impulse, seeing another keg lying on its side, he walked over and righted it.

'As it happens, I'm done with inspecting,' he said, sitting down to face the man. 'Will you spare me a mouthful of what's in your jug? Then mayhap we'll tell each other our troubles.'

'Oh? And what in God's name makes you think I want to hear your troubles?' The other replied, his speech slurring. But on receiving no reply, he leaned forward clumsily and held out the flagon. 'Sir Abel's best sack, from what's left of his store,' he grunted. 'When I was a boy, there would have been wines aplenty there ... enough to feast a great company.'

Revill took the jug, tilted it to his mouth and drank. It was a sweet wine, of good quality. He wiped his mouth and handed it back.

'In truth, I'm surprised you're still here,' Ashman said, frowning at him. 'Haven't you seen enough of

Farthingdown? Didn't I show you all you needed, for your whoreson report?'

At that, Revill stiffened: the man had just given him an idea - an excuse to remain at the manor for a while. The report, of course...

'I thought I would write that up in my chamber, before returning to London,' he said. 'It's peaceful here... no distractions. Might I beg paper and ink from you, and a quill or two?'

The steward gave a shrug and took another drink. 'You've no need to beg, have you? You can command. After what you did for Sir Abel this morning, he'd give you the shirt off his back... that's the sort of fool he is.'

With that, he fell to muttering to himself. Revill caught only a few words – but one of them was plain enough.

'Do you speak of Master Norris?' He enquired. 'I'll confess I'm curious about the man. As a suitor to Lady Charis, I mean-'

'Pah!' With an angry gesture, Ashman cut him short. 'Suitor? Don't play the idiot with me, sir. You'll know as well as I do that the man doesn't care a fig for the girl. Lady Gisela knows it too... it's only her husband and daughter who are too dull-witted to see it!'

'I understood it was a matter of money,' Revill said, choosing his words carefully.

To that the other made no reply, but tilted the flagon to his mouth. Then he set it down heavily, and lifted his gaze.

'Did you, indeed,' he mumbled. 'Well, you may put it in your report, along with any other fancies you can think up. What difference will it make?'

Once again, Revill eyed him. There was an opportunity here, he reasoned, to find out more about the Stanburys – even, perhaps, why Sir Abel might be seen to pose this

A RELUCTANT ASSASSIN

threat that troubled Sir Thomas Heneage enough to want the man dead. He drew a breath, then:

'I asked at dinner about Sir Abel's son, but no-one seemed inclined to talk of him. Lady Gisela said he's on diplomatic duties abroad.'

'Well... so she would,' Ashman nodded vaguely. Then, with a sudden look of suspicion: 'What's he to you, then?'

'Call it idle curiosity,' Revill said. 'Is he the black sheep of the family? He will inherit Farthingdown, will he not, when Sir Abel passes?'

'By the Christ, I hope not! That would be the end of everything... likely the end of me!' Distracted, Ashman looked away – then turned to face Revill with a look of contempt.

'Master Hugh's no diplomat,' he said. 'And I shouldn't tell more... and yet, why should I not? Sir Abel never pays any attention to what I say... you've seen the way he is.' With a lurch he reached down for the flagon at his feet, lifted it, then squinted inside.

'To the devil with him – with all of the Stanburys!' He cried. 'Especially their wastrel son who spies for the Queen, informs even on his fellows, and drives folk to despair with his reprobate ways! What sort of a Master of Farthingdown would he make, Sir Queen's Surveyor, or whatever you are... can you answer me that?'

In surprise, Revill let the words sink in. Hugh Stanbury was an intelligencer? On a sudden, thoughts were crowding his head: Heneage taking over some of Sir Francis Walsingham's duties... his time in Flushing...

'Reprobate ways, you say?' He echoed, after a moment. 'You mean gambling, whoring...?'

'All of those and worse!' The other threw back. 'A scoundrel, in debt up to his ears... there, I've said it!'

'And how do you know he's a spy?' Revill enquired.

'Who doesn't know it?' Came the snarled reply. 'They must be mad over there in the Low Countries – mad or desperate, to think a man like him could do good service. The fellow couldn't keep a secret to save his life. They must have been scraping the barrel.'

Ashman put the flagon to his lips, tilted it upwards to drain the last drop, then dropped it with a thud. He was quite drunk, and Revill sought to use the opportunity. But before he could voice a question, the other levelled a shaky finger at him.

'Do you want to know why that cur Norris is paying court to Lady Charis? I mean, the real reason?' And when Revill showed interest: 'Because of Master Hugh, that's why. They had a wager, and Norris lost the bet! Can you believe that? That's the sort of men they are!'

Though his mind was active, Revill remained impassive. Ashman had stirred more memories in him than he could have known: of men made so reckless by war, half expecting to be killed or maimed at any moment, they would do desperate things - no matter how wild or terrible they might seem to those at home. And if Hugh Stanbury was anything like the man the steward had described, it was quite possible that he would lay such a cruel bet, concerning even his own sister. What struck Revill now was that both he and Turnbull were acquainted, even friends of a sort: here was another link back to Heneage. He was turning it about, when Ashman lurched suddenly to one side and slipped from his seat to the floor.

'Besides,' he grunted, staring blearily up at Revill. 'Even if there was money... even if that rogue Hugh got home safe, and looked to inherit Farthingdown... there'll be naught left. John Cowley's no fool... he'll win his suit, and that'll be the end of it. The case is hopeless... I

A RELUCTANT ASSASSIN

suppose you didn't know that, either. Then, you're just another varlet, that's what you are… you're all varlets…'

His speech failing, the man fell back against the flimsy wall of the hut, which shook as if it would collapse His eyes closed, and soon he was sleeping like a babe.

Revill got up, glanced down at him once, then left him. He stepped outside into a rising wind, took a few paces, then halted.

Two figures were approaching the hut, arm-in-arm – but at sight of him, they stopped abruptly. One was a sturdy maid in plain garb, likely from the Farthingdown kitchens; the other was Tom Bright.

'Ah… Captain – I mean, Master.' He swallowed, assuming a glassy smile. 'I was… er, wondering where you'd got to, so I…'

He broke off: his old commander knew him too well, and a look had appeared that rendered his explanations useless. Allowing his gaze to fall upon the woman, Revill raised an eyebrow, which caused her to flush and make her curtsey.

'This is Mab,' Bright said, somewhat crestfallen. 'She… well, she and I…'

'I regret to disappoint you,' Revill said, 'but the premises are occupied just now.' He jerked his thumb over his shoulder, in the direction of the hut. 'You'll need to find somewhere else to… to converse.'

And with a wry look at his sergeant, he moved off.

SIX

That night after supper, Revill caught Turnbull alone in the hallway and told him to repair to the brewhouse again, within the quarter of an hour.

'And don't disappoint,' he added.

He didn't have long to wait. Quite soon, wearing hat, cloak and sword, the man appeared from the gloom to stop before him, a sour expression on his face. And without wasting time, Revill asked him about Hugh Stanbury and a certain bet he had heard about, that explained his presence here. At that, a scowl appeared.

'By God... what the devil are you're doing?' Turnbull demanded. 'I told you my affairs are naught to you – yet you insist on courting danger!'

'There's no danger to me,' Revill told him. 'In truth, you can't really threaten anyone, can you? Think of the consequences, should Sir Abel be acquainted with your real reasons for this false courtship you pay to his daughter. Not to say, the fact that the money he expects doesn't exist, does it? As jests go, it's as cruel as any I've known.'

For a brief moment, Turnbull looked as if he would put hand to sword-hilt as he had done at their last encounter. But he mastered himself, drawing a long breath.

'Truly, you forget yourself,' he muttered. 'One word from me to Heneage, and you-'

A RELUCTANT ASSASSIN

'You mean, Heneage knows all about your dealings with Sir Abel's son?' Revill broke in. 'I doubt that – nor do I think he'd approve. You're only a jumped-up messenger, are you not? A low-grade snooper. I'll wager Hugh Stanbury's the same – not reliable enough to be trusted with real intelligence work.'

At that Turnbull tensed, raised a finger and pointed it somewhat shakily. 'You over-reach yourself,' he breathed. 'And since you've strayed from your path, damn me if I won't go to Sir Abel and tell him what sort of a man he has under his roof...'

But at Revill's expression he trailed off, a flicker of doubt on his features.

'Odd that you should speak of roofs,' Revill said, with a faint smile. 'After I saved his life this morning, do you really think Sir Abel would believe a word of it? Especially when I mention your relations with his son.'

Disarmed, Turnbull could only glare at him. Moreover, in his anger he seemed to be forgetting Revill's mission, the success of which he was supposed to report. Breathing hard, he sought for some way to recover himself.

'I see one solution to your predicament,' Revill said. He found he was enjoying the other's discomfort, his distaste for the man having hardened to a deep dislike. 'To avoid my exposing you, you could leave on some pretext - disappear, and not return. Lady Charis would be dismayed, of course, but in time her heart would heal. Meanwhile you could report to Heneage that I'd sworn to carry out my mission, so your own work is done.' He raised his eyebrows. 'What say you to that?'

The other merely cursed under his breath.

'And more, while you're in something of a quandary,' Revill went on, 'why not assuage my curiosity? First, is it true about the bet?'

For a moment Turnbull maintained his defiance; then, as if suddenly tired of it all, he appeared to relent. He met Revill's eye, then:

'He hates her.'

Revill blinked, and waited.

'Charis, that is: Hugh hates her, as he loathes and despises his addle-brained father. She was always Sir Abel's favourite, he said - the two of them a pair of dunces. He was in his cups one night – and yes, I took the whoreson bet, and I lost. Now I have to pretend to wed her...'

'Pretend?' Revill broke in. 'You mean, you won't really go through with it?'

'Of course not!' The other retorted. 'Do you think I'm such a fool?' He let out a sigh and lowered his eyes. 'The wedding would be a sham, performed before a hired player posing as a priest. After it's done, I'm to abandon her and leave the letter Hugh gave me. To teach her a lesson, he said... to teach them all a lesson.'

'Well, I almost admire your stamina,' Revill said, after a moment. 'Some might even applaud your diligence, in carrying out the terms of such a wager.'

'You can mock all you like,' Turnbull growled. 'And as to what you said before: Heneage has no illusions about Hugh Stanbury's character. They have an arrangement. So, Master bogus Surveyor, have I satisfied your curiosity now?'

'Not quite,' Revill answered. 'I'll ask you again what I asked you last night: why does Heneage want Sir Abel dead?'

At that, the other hesitated. 'If I told you, what would you do for me in return?'

Revill considered. If he knew the reason why Heneage had blackmailed him into this terrible mission, he reasoned, then he might come at some means of avoiding

A RELUCTANT ASSASSIN

it. He weighed the matter, then said: 'I'll clear the way for you to leave here, without having to go through this sham wedding. You can disappear, and I'll concoct a convincing tale to account for it. As I said before, you can tell Heneage I swore to do what was asked, and you took my word. As for Hugh Stanbury: if you see the man again, you can tell him Charis learned of the deceit and called off the nuptials. Even if he disbelieves you, what can he do?'

Now it was Turnbull's place to consider... whereupon, to Revill's surprise, the man gave a snort of laughter.

'By God,' he murmured. 'Who'd have thought you could be my means of escape from this... mire I've got myself into.' Then, as Revill eyed him, he added: 'Though it's not quite so simple. It's best for all if Charis is married off and out of the way, whoever her unfortunate husband may turn out to be. But in any case...' He paused, then: 'Sir Abel must be removed, so that Hugh inherits Farthingdown - and quickly. Then he and Her Majesty's Vice-Chamberlain can conclude their business.'

'Their business?' Revill echoed, his thoughts wandering. 'What sort of...'

He broke off; Turnbull was nodding.

'You begin to see, I think. On Sir Abel's death by accident, Hugh inherits Farthingdown, then sells off the entire manor to settle his debts - and Heneage gets his share. Charis can marry someone Hugh arranges, and live on in ignorance, while her mother...' he paused, then: 'Her mother, whatever she suspects, can do nothing but live out her days in Charis's new home. While Hugh quits England, likely for ever. He can gamble and roister his way around Europe until he drops dead from drink, or the pox - as if anyone would care.'

'And Heneage's share of the proceeds?' Revill enquired, with some contempt.

'Half, I believe.'

So, there it was. In his mind Revill pictured the elegant, smooth-talking Vice-Chamberlain in his chamber at Walsingham's house, talking of the Queen's safety and the threat a man like Sir Abel might pose, when his chief concern was for a tidy sum of money that would come his way. While he - Revill - was merely an unwitting instrument in Heneage's plans. *The corruptions of office...* the phrase sprang to his mind once again.

'So – I suppose we have a bargain?'

Turnbull's question broke his thoughts. After collecting himself, he managed a nod.

'As soon as you've gone, I'll speak to the family. I'll say you've been called to attend the Court, or some such.'

'You'll need to do better than that,' the other said, with a frown.

'Well, I'll try,' Revill told him. But he was distracted: another matter came to mind, which still pricked his curiosity. 'What of this suit with John Cowley?' He asked, turning the matter about. 'Is it true that Sir Abel will ruin the man, and get his farm? That would add considerably to his wealth, would it not... and to the inheritance?'

'I know little of that,' Turnbull replied, with a shake of his head. 'The lawyer in Weybridge is the one you'd need to ask. Not that he'd tell you anything, I expect.'

He gave a shrug and dropped his gaze. 'Now I think we're finished here, are we not?'

Revill nodded briefly, then watched as the man walked off towards the house.

By the following morning he had cleared his chamber and gone, and Lady Charis was so distraught that she refused to come down to breakfast.

***

A RELUCTANT ASSASSIN

The household was in turmoil: even Leonard Ashman, though seemingly recovered from his drinking-bout the day before, appeared subdued. Perhaps he had forgotten how much he had blurted out, Revill thought briefly. For his own part, he was fully engaged in concocting a pack of lies to account for the sudden disappearance of the Stanburys' future son-in-law.

'I saw him only for a moment, sir,' he told Sir Abel. 'He begged me to make his heartfelt apologies, and to tell you that Lady Charis is forever in his thoughts. But the matter is…' he drew a breath, then: 'He was unwilling to tell you in person, but I'm sure he would understand if I let out a portion of his secret. In short, he-'

'Secret?' Sir Abel broke in, wild-eyed. 'By the Christ, what secret?'

But he was twitching, and it fell to Lady Gisela to take charge. The four of them sat over an unfinished breakfast: the Master of Farthingdown and his wife, Ashman and Revill.

'I pray you, tell us what you can,' she said, meeting Revill's gaze. He stiffened: there was a look in her eye - of suspicion, or something else?

'What I can say is this, my lady,' he replied. 'That there is a deal more to Master… Norris than you knew.' With everyone hanging on his words, he went on: 'You know the kind of service your son performs for Queen and State, and you know that Norris is a compatriot of his. And though he could tell me little, it's my understanding that he received an order to repair at once to London, to receive instructions. He fears he may not return. The… the situation in France, I understand, is most unstable now,' he added, improvising quickly. 'I suspect men like Norris are being recalled at speed.'

'Indeed?' Lady Gisela said frostily. 'And by what means did he receive this order you speak of? By magic?'

'I think a messenger may have come in the night, but I cannot be certain...'

He stopped, ashamed not only of the untruths he had told, but of how feeble they sounded. The other three were gazing at him: Lady Gisela with some suspicion still, Sir Abel in sheer bafflement. Only Ashman, he noticed, seemed unmoved.

'Curious that the servants never mentioned a horseman coming in the night,' he murmured.

Revill said nothing.

'But... you mean, there will be no wedding?' Sir Abel was staring at Revill, as if the import of the matter had only now dawned on him.

'And no money, either,' Ashman said, with some sharpness.

A silence fell. The steward lowered his gaze, but he had spoken the truth. Revill glanced at Lady Gisela, who to his surprise appeared somewhat relieved. Finally, she looked round at the three men, and seemed to come to a decision.

'Well then, we must adjust,' she said firmly. 'Cut our coat according to our cloth – which means, first and foremost, giving up all notions of hosting the Queen on her Progress next summer. I believe Master Revill will confirm my opinion in that – will you not, sir?'

After a moment, Revill nodded. 'One must face the facts of the matter, Sir Abel,' he said, turning to his host. 'As I tried to tell you, the expense would be prohibitive-'

'Damn and blast the expense!'

Startling everyone, Sir Abel banged a hand down on the table, so hard that his plate and cup jumped from the board. 'I told you... I swore to you...' he was gazing fiercely at Revill. 'My lawsuit with Cowley will yield results – and

A RELUCTANT ASSASSIN

whatever shortfall remains can be made up by means of loans! I'm not entirely without influence at Court... I had friends, even Sir Francis Walsingham was among them! How much higher can you go than that?'

He turned to stare angrily at his wife. He was shaking, and a spasm seemed inevitable. Since no-one else seemed willing to find the words, Revill cleared his throat.

'I should tell you that Sir Francis is a very sick man nowadays, sir,' he said. 'They say he may die within months - perhaps sooner.'

'But, your report... your survey,' Sir Abel faltered. 'You can mention the moneys due from Cowley, can you not? Not to mention the repairs I'm already making to the house – you've seen them yourself. By next summer you won't recognise the place, I just know it-'

'For pity's sake, Sir Abel!'

It was Ashman who cried out, stopping him in midflow. Taut as a post, the man seemed to have lost his habitual self-control, and was gazing fiercely at his master. 'This is but foolishness, sir – you clutch at straws,' he added hurriedly. 'I beg you, view the matter as it is, and not through some coloured glass. Whatever may come of the suit with Cowley, it cannot fund the hosting of the Queen along with the great press of her people – even if we had the room! The surveyor...' he turned swiftly for support. 'The surveyor knows the truth of it, sir – and he will make full report. Is that not so?'

As one, they looked at Revill. After glancing at Lady Gisela, who had raised her eyebrows in anticipation, he faced Sir Abel and gave a nod.

'It's true, sir,' he said. 'I regret that I can only recommend to my masters that Farthingdown is unsuitable and should not be included on Her Majesty's list of destinations.'

There followed another silence. Ashman lifted his cup and took a drink, avoiding all eyes. While Lady Gisela made no attempt to hide her relief: the matter was out in the open at last, and could not be plainer. She met Revill's eye approvingly.

'So... so, that's what your report will say, is it not?' Sir Abel said, after a pause. 'The report you will pen under my roof, I understand – with paper and ink supplied by my steward.'

He was gazing at Revill with a look of mingled sadness and hurt. 'While you continue to enjoy my hospitality, and walk about my gardens,' he went on, 'and all the while you've merely indulged me. Tolerated my hopes as if I were a fool, and-'

'He also saved your life,' Lady Gisela broke in, in a dry tone. 'Or had you forgotten?'

Her husband drew a long breath, and held it in. Expecting a spasm, the others tensed – but instead he exhaled and put his hands on the table to steady himself.

'Then I'll ask but one thing more of you - sir,' he said, with an effort. 'That before you finish your report, you go to my lawyer in Weybridge and ask him how goes the suit with Cowley. I will give you a letter to carry, authorising him to answer your questions. His name is Thomas Aubridge. Will you at least do that for me... Master Surveyor?'

Whereupon he merely gazed at Revill, who could see no other course.

'Of course, Sir Abel,' he answered. 'I will leave as soon as you furnish me with your letter.' And with that he rose, made a brief obeisance, and said he would make preparations.

A RELUCTANT ASSASSIN

A short time later, having gone to the stable to attend to Malachi, he found Tom Bright grooming the horse. As he entered, the sergeant looked round cheerfully enough.

'I thought I'd give this fellow a good rub down, Captain,' he ventured. 'Seeing as no-one else has shifted their arse to do it.'

'That's well.' Revill threw him a brief smile, though his heart was heavy. 'In fact, I must ride into Weybridge soon...' then, as the notion struck him: 'Do you want to come along? Quit this place for a while... this *Falling-down*, as you say the servants name it? I'll buy you a dinner.'

'A splendid idea, is that,' Bright said at once.

'And speaking of servants,' Revill said, 'I'd urge some restraint where young Mab is concerned. We're not likely to be here much longer.'

'Indeed?' Bright's grin faded. 'Ah, well... all things must pass.' He eyed his master for a moment. 'Your surveying business all done, then... if that's what it was?'

Revill barely nodded and changed the subject.

An hour later, with Sir Abel's letter in his pocket, he rode Malachi out of the gates of Farthingdown with his sergeant bringing up the rear on the hired jennet, the two of them commencing the short distance downriver to the village of Weybridge.

He had no relish whatsoever for the visit to his host's lawyer, for it would change nothing. But in his mind's eye he saw again the look of near-desperation on the old knight's face, and was moved to pity him. Whereupon once again, the burden of his mission fell upon him, and almost made him droop in the saddle.

He knew now that, whatever the consequences, he could no more kill that troubled old man than he could put to death one of his own kinfolk. How he was to resolve that predicament, however, was shrouded in an impenetrable fog.

SEVEN

It was a Friday, and Weybridge was lively enough. Having found stabling for the horses near the little church of St Nicholas, the two men parted in the street: Revill to walk to the house of the lawyer, and Bright to spend his time as he pleased. There was an inn close by, where they would take dinner.

'And don't get soused,' Revill said, as his sergeant walked off.

It was but a short distance to Thomas Aubridge's home, an imposing enough dwelling on the northern side of the village, near the river. Having been admitted by a servant, he stood in a hallway until a door opened, and the lawyer appeared in his formal gown: a corpulent, clean-shaven man of pinkish complexion. Having given his name, Revill handed him Sir Abel's letter. After breaking the seal and glancing at it, he looked up with a frown.

'What in God's name does he want now?' He demanded. 'And what, pray, is your interest, sir?'

Revill mentioned his commission, and added something about needing to know the value and condition of Farthingdown Manor, including such matters as debts and monies due.

'And that's all, is it?'

But when Revill merely raised his eyebrows and waited, the other gave a sigh and turned towards the open door, telling him he had better come in.

Once inside his private chamber, which was stuffy and lined with shelves of books and rolled papers, the man retreated behind his table and sat down, gesturing Revill to a joined stool nearby. Having cleared aside some documents, he spread Sir Abel's letter out before him, donned a pair of thick spectacles and read it through.

'So, Master... Revill,' he intoned, looking up. 'What is it you wish to know?'

'I'd like to know about the lawsuit betwixt Sir Abel and his neighbour, John Cowley,' Revill told him. 'What I've heard thus far is somewhat confusing.'

'Indeed?' The other frowned again. 'I'd have thought it was as plain as a pikestaff.'

'You mean, Sir Abel's case is sound? He will gain the land he was promised?'

'Eh? By God, I mean no such thing!' Aubridge wore a pained look. 'Quite the reverse. It's Cowley who is in the right – I've tried to explain it a dozen times, but...' he spread his hands helplessly. 'It's like talking to a statue - one that can't keep still for a minute.'

Taken aback, Revill turned the matter over. In his mind's eye he saw Sir Abel talking airily of the suit which would enrich him - was that but an illusion? Another of the Master of Farthingdown's fantasies? After a pause, he mentioned the matter of the late Samuel Cowley and his gratitude towards Sir Abel's father for saving his life – only to receive a scornful reply.

'Oh, that old tale!' Aubridge gave a groan and clapped his hands to his fleshy face. But after a moment he lowered them, faced Revill and shook his head.

'Old Cowley was the worst skinflint I've ever known,' he said with a sigh. 'He'd not give you the sweepings of his stables - let alone a piece of good pasture! And Sir Abel's father - Sir Walter Stanbury, I mean - was an unworldly soul who'd believe anything he was told. Even if he had saved his neighbour from drowning when they were boys – what of it?'

'But, the will...' Revill frowned. 'I was told Samuel Cowley changed it before he died, and the old one was lost - which sounded a little suspicious to me.'

'It is not suspicious,' Aubridge retorted. 'The old rogue did indeed change his will, so I understand - but not to Sir Abel's benefit. It was merely to cut out his nephew, who was claiming a share in the farm.' He paused, blinking through his spectacles. 'There never was any land to be added to the Farthingdown acres – and that, sir, is the nub of the matter.'

'Then, why does the suit drag on?' Revill demanded. 'Surely as Sir Abel's lawyer, you should disabuse him of this illusion he harbours...'

But he broke off: the other had lowered his gaze, looking somewhat embarrassed. From what he knew of lawyers, this man could simply be dragging out the case to fatten his fees. He was forming another question – until Aubridge spoke up with some heat.

'In heaven's name, can you not guess?' He demanded. 'I've known the Stanburys all my life – do you think I want to see Sir Abel ruined? If I bring the case to the Courts he will lose, whereupon Cowley will issue a countersuit for defamation and God knows what else! Do you not think the family has troubles enough?'

To that Revill made no answer; he believed he knew the truth when he heard it. And hence, his spirits sinking, he saw little reason for remaining here. The thought of relaying what he now knew to Sir Abel filled him with gloom. On a sudden, he was chastising himself not only for getting caught up in the Stanburys' affairs, but for going to Farthingdown in the first place - though the means by which he had been forced were ever present, like an immoveable rock. He drew a long breath, looked up and found Thomas Aubridge's eyes upon him.

'Pardon me, Revill,' he said, in a different tone. 'You spoke of suspicion, and I'll be plain with you. What strikes me as suspicious is the notion of a man like you being sent by Her Majesty's Surveyor of Works, to assess Farthingdown as a suitable place for the Queen to visit on her summer progress. In truth, I find it most unlikely.'

'Do you?' Revill met his eye. 'Well, that's your opinion. And I'm uncertain what you mean by *a man like me*.'

'Then let me be plainer still,' the other said. 'Half of Surrey knows that Farthingdown is in a poor condition, as it knows of Sir Abel's madness...' seeing Revill's expression, he lifted a hand. 'Pray, let me continue. Many are also of the opinion that the man's only hope is to see his daughter married to a person of substance.' He puffed out his cheeks. 'There have been suitors, of course, but none who stayed the course... the latest is a man named Norris-'

'He's gone,' Revill said, cutting his short. 'And unlikely to return.'

Aubridge blinked. 'What do you mean?'

'I mean that the wedding will not take place,' Revill said.

'Well... I confess I'm relieved to hear that,' the other replied, after a moment. 'I never trusted that man,' he added quickly. 'Sir Abel is... shall I say, of a somewhat trusting nature.'

'Unlike Lady Gisela,' Revill put in.

Aubridge regarded him for a while, then looked away. To Revill's eye, the man's mood appeared to have lightened considerably.

A RELUCTANT ASSASSIN

'Perhaps it's time I paid a visit to the Stanbury seat myself,' he said. 'But let me return to what I said concerning your arrival there, ostensibly to inspect the manor. In short, sir, I don't believe a word of it.'

Revill met his eye, but gave no answer.

'Hence, I find myself speculating as to why you're really at Farthingdown. Might it be…' he hesitated, then: 'Could it be that you harbour intentions towards Lady Charis yourself?'

'Your pardon… are you serious?' Revill replied - whereupon the truth struck him. And quite quickly, he found himself trying not to laugh.

'Let me reassure you, sir, that I have no such intentions,' he said, clearing his throat. 'And I'm in agreement that a visit to Farthingdown would be a prudent move on your part. I believe Lady Charis is in sore need of comfort, just now.'

Their eyes met, before Aubridge looked away quickly. There was little doubt in Revill's mind now that the man had hopes of his own towards the Stanbury daughter… whereupon another notion struck him.

'And might it not be a good time to acquaint Sir Abel with the true condition of his suit against Cowley?' He suggested, raising his eyebrows. 'Surely he must learn the truth of it sooner or later?'

But at that, the other's face fell. 'I fear it would finish him,' he said. 'Now that Norris is gone, his case is…' he paused. 'It's Lady Gisela I pity most,' he added, with a sigh. 'She has suffered a good deal…. and as for her wayward son…'

He was distracted, shaking his head. He barely noticed that his visitor had risen, hat in hand, and was looking down at him.

'I'll tell Sir Abel what I've learned,' Revill said, and moved promptly to the door.

Once outside the house, he glanced up to see rain clouds gathering and pulled his cloak about him. One thing was uppermost in his thoughts: he should take his leave from Farthingdown, perhaps this very day, then try to find some escape from the bind he was in. The notion of riding directly to Devon returned: he could warn Katherine and her husband, perhaps help them to move elsewhere - even to quit England, for a country where they would not live in fear because of their religion. Just then he saw no other course – apart from his immediate need for a pipe and a cup of something strong. Quickening his pace, he walked through the village towards the inn.

He had almost reached the doorway when from nowhere a small, barefoot boy in humble garb appeared, blocking his way.

'Are you the captain, sir?' He piped.

Revill blinked, taking in his ragged appearance.

'He said you was his captain - you wore a cloak, and you had a scar on your right hand... the sergeant, that is,' the lad went on quickly. 'Tis you, is it not?'

'Let's say it is,' Revill said, after a pause. 'Do you have a message for me, or...?'

'He's waiting at the stables,' the other broke in. 'He said you'd best come quick.'

'Oh? Why is that?' Revill wanted to know.

'Stone me if I know why, sir,' came the reply. 'But he gave me a halfpenny to wait for you at the inn and tell you. So now I've earned it, I'll be off-'

He yelped, as Revill's hand shot out to seize him by the arm.

A RELUCTANT ASSASSIN

'Why is he in the stable?' He demanded, leaning down so that the boy flinched. 'And is he alone? You're not going until you've told me.'

'Peace, master!' The lad was squirming. 'I swear, I don't know aught but what I've said!'

'Is he alone?' Revill repeated, tightening his grip.

But at that moment, the door of the inn swung open, and a man stepped out clumsily, to stop at sight of the two of them in his path. It was all the ragged boy needed: with lightning speed he kicked Revill hard on the shin, making him loosen his grip. The next moment he had torn himself free, darted aside and was running off up the street.

When Revill grunted and leaned down to rub his leg, the customer regarded him blearily.

'Looks like rain again, does it not?' He enquired.

But without replying, Revill walked off towards the stables where Malachi and Bright's jennet were housed. A sixth sense had kicked in: he could almost smell a ruse. By the time he had reached the building, he had thrown aside hat and cloak and unsheathed his sword.

And in less than a minute, battle was drawn.

A quick entrance was best, he knew: no tentative pushing open of doors. He threw one door wide, stepped into the gloom with its smell of hay and horses, and dropped to a crouch – just as a shout came from some yards away:

'At your back! There's three of them-'

It was Tom Bright, now letting out a muffled cry as his mouth was stopped. But by instinct Revill ducked aside – and heard the hiss of air as a blade flew past his ear. Turning rapidly, he made a feint with his sword, seeing a surprisingly short man facing him, the lower half of his face covered with a scarf. This one jerked backwards, recovered his balance and prepared to strike anew - just as a rustle of straw came from directly behind Revill. He ducked again, whirled about and sliced the air – to be rewarded with a yelp of pain as his blade connected.

But there was no time to think. He barely had a moment to swing his sword back before, with a clash of steel, his first assailant's blade met the edge of his. He staggered: the short man was stronger than he looked. Whereupon, without a word spoken, the two of them fell to sword-play – only this was no fencing hall: the fight was for life and limb.

Three of them, Bright had said... aware that he was severely disadvantaged, since it seemed the sergeant was in no position to aid him, Revill steeled himself and went into combat. He could not afford to consider the man he had wounded; he believed he had heard him fall, but could not be certain. He concentrated on parrying his opponent's thrusts before finding his opportunity - and mercifully, it was not slow in coming.

For, as he soon realised, the other man was no match for him: squat and thick-legged, he relied more on strength than on skill. Revill allowed himself to be forced backwards by a few lunges, giving the impression he was weakening, and finally, appearing to lose his balance. Seeing his chance, the other closed in, sword-arm raised – and was too slow to see Revill's poniard, which came up from nowhere and was driven hard between his ribs.

The stocky man froze, as a wheeze escaped his lips. His sword arm dropped... as did his eyes, to gaze down forlornly at the welter of blood gushing from his innards. Then his knees went, and he folded like an empty sack – just as another commotion broke out.

'Captain! To your left-'

It was Bright, his cry cut short once again. His shout was followed by the sounds of a scuffle... Revill whirled

A RELUCTANT ASSASSIN

about, squinting in the poor light, and believed he saw his sergeant engaged in a tussle with a taller figure. The stable lanterns had been doused, he thought fleetingly. He glimpsed horses, stamping nervously in their stalls – and then he acted.

Rapier in his right hand, poniard in his left, he dropped like a stone and swerved aside on the straw-strewn floor – just as a sword descended with force, slicing into his left upper arm. Thanks to his evasive move it was a glancing blow, yet his doublet was slashed, and pain followed: a sharp, burning spasm. Breathing hard, he sprang to his feet, knowing that the man he had wounded earlier was up and upon him... and this one was mad with rage.

Hissing with pain, one wrist dripping blood and the scarf slipping from his face, he loomed over Revill, bent on the final act. His blade rose again and fell at speed, but Revill met it with his sword-hilt, though the force almost knocked him sideways. Recovering quickly, he lunged with his poniard – but the other batted it aside, sending it flying from his hand.

Breathless and hurting, half-crouching, the two of them faced each other.

It was harder this time: the man was taller and leaner, and a better swordsman than his companion, who was likely bleeding his last. But at the back of Revill's mind as they fought and weaved, blades clashing in the dusty stable, was the existence of a third man, who had seemingly been watching over Tom Bright – and who seemed to have overpowered him. He heard his sergeant cursing aloud: likely he had been bound when the trap was laid, and the ragged boy sent to bring Revill here...

Someone wanted him dead - and just now, there seemed to be a fair chance they would get their wish.

He made a rapid forward thrust, which the other parried – but as he did so his other hand in its blood-soaked sleeve swung out, to crack Revill on the cheek. Droplets of blood flew from the wrist, spattering Revill's face. Worse, one landed in his eye... darting aside, he lashed out with his free hand and connected with his opponent's jaw. The man spluttered a curse, of pain and desperation; both of them were weakening, and both knew it. And still, Revill was steeled for the third assailant to arrive...

But he didn't.

There came a cry of agony from the other end of the stable, followed by the sound of someone falling heavily. Whereupon, to Revill's huge relief, the noise was followed by a familiar voice, and footsteps stumbling towards him.

'I'm here, Captain!'

The result was confusion for Revill's opponent. His head snapped round, even as his arm flew up – but it was time enough. Without hesitating Revill thrust his rapier cleanly into the man's chest, putting all his weight behind it. Then he stepped back, placed his foot on the other's body and withdrew the blade, producing a fountain of gore. At the same moment Bright appeared in his eyeline, hands tied before him, gripping a poniard awkwardly between them as if he were about to chop firewood. Stopping dead, he let out a gasp.

But it was over. Dying even as he dropped to the floor, the swordsman crumpled in a heap. Revill took another step back and looked round quickly. Tom Bright followed his gaze, to where the first of the two who had waylaid him lay senseless, in a puddle of blood.

'Fuck me, Captain,' was all he could find to say.

Revill looked at him, one eye blurred and stinging. He dropped his own sword, blinked and put a hand to his face. Then he tensed abruptly, glancing round.

A RELUCTANT ASSASSIN

'No – there's no need to fret about the other one,' Bright said, jerking a thumb over his shoulder. 'He thought he had me trammelled, but I got my knee in his cods, then gave him a kicking. He'll have trouble standing up, for sure.'

'Are you hurt?' Revill muttered, still recovering his breath.

'Only my pride,' came the reply. 'Took me for a proper fool, they did...' he glanced round. 'Knew who I was, too. Brought me here and tied me while they sent for you. I saw them before they covered their faces...' he shrugged. 'Not that it matters, now.'

Then he stiffened, squinting at Revill. 'Sweet Jesus, you need a surgeon quick.'

'I know, Tom.' Stiffly Revill began to unbutton his doublet, then paused. 'Hadn't I better cut your hands free?'

It was done quickly, with the dagger Bright had taken from his captor: the man who was now sitting up some distance away, grunting with pain. With one eye on the fellow, the sergeant and Revill got the doublet off between them and examined the gash in his upper arm, which was bleeding heavily. No stranger to battle wounds, Bright tore the sleeve off Revill's shirt and tied a makeshift tourniquet. Finally, with a glance at one another, they stepped away from the lifeless bodies and bore down upon the third man, who flinched at their approach.

He was masked like the others, but from his clothes he was no hired ruffian, as Revill guessed the others were. When he and Bright stood over him, he raised his head balefully. But Revill frowned: was there something familiar about him? Stooping quickly, he reached down and tore the scarf away roughly... then straightened at once.

With a savage look, his face pale as ashes, Lewis Turnbull gazed up at him.

EIGHT

This was neither the time nor place for an interrogation. The ostler who kept the stables had been paid to disappear for an hour and would return soon. This became known when Bright held a poniard to Turnbull's neck, telling him that he would need little excuse to slit his gizzard. Revill knew it was a bluff and played his own part accordingly.

'I can plead self-defence,' he said, squatting down before the former suitor of Lady Charis, who was now his prisoner, his sword and poniard taken from him. 'Given the odds – and my status as a servant of the Crown, of course – I expect to be believed. Whereas you…' he shook his head. 'With your mask back on and hands tied, you'll look like a villain bent on robbery. And with your tongue cut out, you won't be able to offer much of a defence.' He turned to his sergeant. 'You can do it clean, like you did to that Spaniard once, can't you?'

'With pleasure,' Bright muttered.

'So…' Revill eyed their captive again. 'Tell me why you set this snare, and we'll leave you to deal with the shambles it's caused. You and your silky tongue - you'll think of something.'

Turnbull opened his mouth, took a breath, then closed it again.

'I'll ask once more,' Revill informed him. 'Why did you try to have me killed? If you don't answer, I won't wait any longer.' He half-turned to Bright, who without

A RELUCTANT ASSASSIN

prompting pressed the blade harder to the man's throat. At the same time, he seized Turnbull's hair with his other hand and yanked his head back, making him cry out.

'By Jesus, enough!' He shouted. And when the other two merely waited, he cursed under his breath. But his case was hopeless, and he knew it.

'Heneage's orders!' He spat, his eyes on Revill. 'Once you'd despatched Sir Abel, I was to despatch you. And I wish to God I had!'

Revill stiffened - and then he understood. Of course, Heneage would want no-one left alive who might speak of his own treachery... perhaps even Turnbull's days were numbered, he thought briefly. With a glance at Bright, who looked stunned on a sudden, he got slowly to his feet, painfully aware of the throbbing from his wound.

'Even though you knew I hadn't carried out the task?' He enquired. 'Were you even prepared to return later, and do it yourself?' He let out a breath. 'Well now, Heneage must surely have a tight hold over you.' And when Turnbull merely cursed him, he added: 'You had me watched, I suppose? Was it one of those two?'

He meant the dead assailants, to which the man's silence suggested he had guessed aright.

'We'd best be gone, Captain.'

Bright had stood up abruptly, glancing towards the doors. 'Someone will come.'

'You can get your horse,' Revill said. But as the sergeant moved off towards the stalls, he leaned down to eye Turnbull one last time.

'I wouldn't go back to Heneage now if I were you,' he said. 'You know he doesn't like failure. I'd find a boatman to carry me down the Thames to Deptford, then take ship for France. But you'll please yourself.'

Turnbull met his gaze, but had no words.

And a short time later, as he got painfully to his feet, he could only watch with smouldering rage as the man he had been ordered to kill led his horse from the stable, behind his servant. From the look in his eye, there would be a reckoning.

Just then a distant roll of thunder sounded, and a heavy rain began to fall.

***

Revill and Bright moved quickly through the village in the downpour, Revill covering his injured arm with his cloak. When they turned down an alley, he got rid of Turnbull's sword and poniard. Then he waited with the horses while his sergeant hurried off to find a barber-surgeon. Thankfully he was back a few minutes later, saying there was one not far away. Soaking wet, they led the mounts to the house, where a thatched lean-to offered temporary shelter. But when Revill started for the door, the sergeant hung back.

'I'll watch the animals,' he said shortly.

Their eyes met, whereupon Revill gave a sigh.

'I wanted to tell you, about Sir Abel. I swear, if I didn't have compelling reasons…'

'Your wound must be stitched,' the other broke in. 'Then back to Farthingdown, and rest.'

He looked away, busying himself with tightening the jennet's saddle. Meanwhile, Malachi eyed his master with what looked uncannily like an expression of reproach.

With a sigh Revill went inside the house, where the barber-surgeon's wife greeted him briefly and brought him into the front parlour.

The surgeon was elderly, a few wisps of white hair on his mottled scalp. When Revill removed his wet cloak, the man took in his appearance without a word and gestured

A RELUCTANT ASSASSIN

him to a stool. Having sat down heavily, he was about to speak when the other stayed him.

'There's no need for explanations, sir,' he said, in a gruff voice. 'I know a sword-cut when I see one. My fee to clean the wound, sew it and bandage it is one shilling. Discretion will cost you another shilling.'

'How much discretion does that buy?' Revill enquired; suddenly, he felt very tired.

'Enough,' came the terse reply. 'Provided I never see you again. I'll also give you a pad soaked in clove oil, against the pain.'

And so, with a nod he put himself in the hands of this man as he went to work with practised skill. And a half hour later, weak from loss of blood and the pain of the stitches, he emerged from the house in his stained doublet, to find Bright standing with both horses saddled.

Throughout their ride back to Farthingdown, not a word was said.

***

On arriving at the manor, Revill made up a tale about a fall from his horse in the rain, having mudded his cloak to add substance to it. Needing to rest and recover, he retired to his chamber where water for washing was sent in. Soon afterwards, food and a cup of wine were brought by a servant: none other than Mab, whose relations with Tom Bright he now recalled. Somewhat to his surprise, the young maid was cheerfully talkative.

'That lane's full of potholes, sir,' she told him. 'It must be God's mercy that folk don't fall every day. Not that we get visitors every day. You and Tom – Master Bright, I mean – are the first in a long while.' She set the tray on a chest by the wall, and turned to face him. 'Apart from Master Norris, that is…' she let out a sigh. 'Poor Lady

Charis is beside herself, now he's gone. She's away to her cousin at Camberley. Needs a change of air, she says.'

Revill took in the news, sitting on the edge of the bed. But when he enquired whether Mab had seen Tom Bright, she shook her head.

'Like a drowned cat when he came in, wasn't he? That's what I heard.' She hesitated, then: 'Begging your pardon, sir, but will you be staying longer at Farthingdown? Only, there's been gossip – then, there always is.' She put on a grin. 'Not much happens here as a rule.'

'So I've discovered, Mab,' Revill replied. 'It's but a matter of my penning a report. I expect we'll be gone before the weekend is done.'

At that, her face fell. 'Is it so?' She sighed. 'Ah, well-a-day.'

'Are Sir Abel and Lady Gisela at their dinner just now?'

'So they are, sir. Lady Gisela was most sorry to hear of your mishap. She hopes you'll be well enough to come down to supper.'

Revill gave a brief nod, whereupon Mab bobbed and left the room. As she went out, she glanced back to see him stretch out on the bed and close his eyes.

Thereafter he slept until nightfall, his dinner untouched.

***

When he entered the dining-chamber that evening in a fresh shirt, his doublet cleaned and mended by the washerwoman, he found Lady Gisela already at table, sipping from her silver cup. He murmured a greeting, made his bow, then he sat down without expression. Then Leonard Ashman came in, glanced at him and took his seat without a word. A servant came forward with the wine jug, and another entered the room bearing a huge platter of roast meats. Whereupon the Mistress of Farthingdown lowered her cup and gazed at Revill over the rim.

A RELUCTANT ASSASSIN

'I'm relieved to see you recovered, sir,' she murmured. 'A shoulder injury, was it not?'

'Indeed... I'm a little restored now, my lady,' Revill said.

'That's well.' She glanced at Ashman, who was helping himself from the platter. 'I would ask about your visit to Aubridge, but we should wait for Sir Abel...' she paused. 'He's somewhat in the dumps, hence I'll ask once again for your understanding.'

'Of course,' Revill said, his heart heavy. The news he had to impart – and he was resolved to tell the plain truth – would likely send the old knight's spirits plunging even further. And yet, when the man himself came in a moment later, he was surprised to see him in apparent calm humour.

'I'm pleased to find you at table,' he said. 'Was your shoulder put out? I can have someone attend to it.'

'Nay, Sir Abel.' Revill managed a faint smile. 'Just a strain, and bruises... it will mend soon enough.'

'Indeed? Eat well, then. And after, you may report what Aubridge has said.'

A servant having pulled back his chair, he sat down and held out his cup to be filled. And though the tension among the others at table was palpable, the Master of Farthingdown seemed not to notice. Soon he was dining heartily, with hardly a twitch and none of his frequent outbursts. Revill began to suspect that the man was making a powerful effort to appear relaxed. Finally, after most of the meal had been consumed in silence, Sir Abel pushed away his platter. Lady Gisela, meanwhile, had barely touched her food. Raising her eyes, she looked at Revill, who took this for a sign that he should proceed.

'My visit to Aubridge this morning was somewhat brief, sir,' he began, turning to his host. 'And in truth, though I wish it were otherwise, I do not bring good news. The matter is-'

'Saints and demons!'

Sir Abel's shout cut him short, sending a wave of alarm round the seated company. The two manservants standing nearby backed to the wall, eyes averted, while Lady Gisela sighed audibly and took a drink. Only Ashman appeared unmoved, paying great attention to a dish of candied fruits. Meanwhile the head of the table struggled to master his spasm, swivelling his head. At last, after fortifying himself with a gulp of wine, he eyed Revill.

'The matter is?' He echoed, as if nothing had occurred.

Whereupon, when even Ashman lifted his gaze Revill drew a breath and gave Sir Abel his account of what the lawyer had said, leaving out only those parts which would insult him. It took a very few minutes, for there was little to tell. And though he refrained from repeating Aubridge's exact words – *there never was any land to add to the Farthingdown acres* – the conclusion was clear and stark. When he had finished, he took a fortifying drink himself and awaited the outcome.

At first, there was silence; then Ashman threw Revill a glance of approval and faced his master.

'There it is in a nutshell, sir,' he said with a sigh. 'In truth, I've always suspected as much – and in your heart, I believe you have too.'

There was no answer. Lady Gisela dabbed her mouth with a napkin and looked as if she were about to speak – and then came the explosion.

'Liar!'

In a trice, Sir Abel leaped to his feet, sending his chair crashing to the floor behind him. With an angry cry he lashed out, sending his cup and platter flying from the table. Stretching forward, he seized Revill's cup and threw

A RELUCTANT ASSASSIN

it against the wall, red wine splashing across the oak panels like blood. And when Revill rose involuntarily, the man stepped away from the table and levelled a shaking finger at him.

'You lie, sir!' He cried. 'You're a rogue like the rest of them – you and Aubridge, and Cowley, and that sweet-voiced varlet Norris – you conspire against me! Devils, all of you! You want to ruin me... drive me into my grave, so you can divide my lands – even that wastrel son of mine will have his way! I see you, what you are... and I won't bear it!'

He paused, trembling, his gaze straying to Lady Gisela, who remained seated. Though shaken, she maintained an air of calm as she said: 'It's clear that our guest's tidings are a shock, sir. Will you go to your chamber and rest? I'll have a physic prepared-'

'And you, madam – you're a part of it!'

Wild-eyed now, her husband took a step towards her - upon which, fearing some assault, the men reacted. Ashman stood up, gesturing to the servants to come forward. Meanwhile, on impulse, Revill put himself between Sir Abel and his wife.

'Peace, sir,' he murmured, lifting his hands slightly. 'I strove only to tell the truth, harsh as it may be... when you're calm, you may come to see it as a blessing, in a way-'

'Blessing?! By God...'

Beside himself, the old knight dropped a hand to his waist. But he wore no sword, nor any other weapon. Looking about him, he began twitching again... he even staggered slightly, prompting Revill to come forward to aid him. At the same time the servants hurried up, one on either side of their master, and took him gently by the elbows.

'I pray you, sir – for my sake if no other – go and rest.'

Lady Gisela, on her feet now, was looking anxiously at her husband. For a moment their eyes met... then all at once, Sir Abel sagged. To the alarm of the watchers his eyes rolled, his mouth fell open and spittle ran from it. He swayed, his weight supported by the servants with difficulty, until Revill moved to help them despite his wound. Thereafter, without ceremony, the Master of Farthingdown was taken out, Ashman following close behind.

Between them the men half-carried him up the staircase to the first floor, past tattered hangings, to his curtained chamber. There he was made comfortable in his old four-poster bed, while candles were lit and word sent to the kitchens to prepare a posset. But once Sir Abel's head was on the pillow, a weariness seemed to overpower him. With a few muttered words that nobody understood, he fell into a sleep.

In silence, Revill and Ashman descended and returned to Lady Gisela, who had resumed her seat at the table. Someone had retrieved the fallen cups and platter and done a hasty job of wiping down the panelling, and a servant was pouring wine. Subdued, Ashman told his mistress that her husband was sleeping, and that someone would watch over him throughout the night. A physician would be summoned in the morning. Whereupon the lady bade him sit and threw him a cool look, before facing Revill.

'I can only ask your pardon, madam,' he said, as he took his seat. 'I should have found a way to sugar the pill, perhaps...'

But Lady Gisela stayed him. 'No... you spoke the truth, and it had to be done. Indeed...' she hesitated, then: 'It should have been done long ago. That man – Aubridge, I mean – is a craven coward. He always feared Sir Abel, and

A RELUCTANT ASSASSIN

used any excuse not to come here. But I knew the substance of it, and so did my steward. It needed someone from outside – a man of authority such as yourself, who has earned his trust, to break the news.'

This was said with a frown at Ashman, who was lifting his cup. But instead of drinking, he met her eye and sighed.

'I believe this moment was destined, my lady - and likely the arrival of Her Majesty's Surveyor was the catalyst that brought it about. You said it yourself: we at Farthingdown must cut our coat accordingly. Indeed…' he paused, then appeared to gird himself. 'Is this not the time to accept that Sir Abel is too unwell to run the manor as he once did?'

Lady Gisela kept eyes on him, her frown deepening. 'What mean you by that, Master Steward?' She asked sharply.

'What I mean, madam, is that you should take the reins yourself,' came the equally sharp reply. 'You already manage the household. Between us, we can make a proper examination of Farthingdown's condition – its debts and assets – and take what action is necessary. Beginning…' He drew a breath, and put down his cup. 'Beginning with our putting an end to this foolish suit against Cowley, which can bring nothing but ruin.'

A silence followed. Wearied by it all, Revill wanted to excuse himself. But his thoughts strayed: to the fight in the stable, the two masked men lying in their own blood; to Turnbull's subsequent, bitter confession; to the look of dismay on Tom Bright face, now that the true reason for their coming here was out; then back to Heneage in London, telling him how he had no choice in the matter of his mission - and finally to Jenna, awaiting his return in ignorance of the whole tawdry affair.

He realised then that he had barely thought of her in days. With a sigh, he shook himself out of his reverie, and realised someone was addressing him.

'I said, are you ill, sir?' Lady Gisela asked, her eyes upon him.

'Your pardon, my lady,' he murmured. 'I ache somewhat, and my mind had drifted.'

'Of course... your shoulder,' she nodded. 'You must retire. Is there anything you need?'

With a polite refusal, Revill got to his feet and wished her and her steward good night. Before leaving, however, he spoke of finishing his report the next day; it would give him time not only to rest but to think. Thereafter, he got himself up the stairs, and with relief closed the door to his chamber. Sinking down on the bed, his wound throbbing with pain, he let out a sigh and gazed down at the floor.

One thing, at least, was plain enough now: his sojourn at Farthingdown was over.

As soon as he felt able to make the journey back to London – perhaps the next day, or the one after, he thought - he would leave. Though whether Tom Bright would be accompanying him was in doubt. At the very least, he owed his loyal sergeant – a man who would follow him into the very jaws of hell - a full explanation. Thereafter he would return to Jenna... and when he was fully recovered, he would face Heneage; beyond that, he dared not think.

But some hours later – perhaps only one or two, he was unsure – he awoke in his bed with a start. The room was pitch dark, and yet he was alert at once, thinking he had heard a sound – then came the scrape of a tinder-box, and a flame sprang up.

'Who's there?' He called out, sitting up quickly. He no longer slept with a poniard under his pillow, and would

A RELUCTANT ASSASSIN

have cursed himself for his carelessness – until a female voice sounded from beyond the glare of the candle.

'Calm yourself, sir. I mean no harm.'

He stiffened, peering into the wavering light as it approached - then drew a breath. Barely a yard away, Lady Gisela stood in a white shift, her hair unbound. With a steady hand she raised the candle, peering into his face.

'I've no wish to alarm you,' she said. 'Nor to give the wrong impression - I'm a faithful spouse, and no Jezebel.' But when Revill merely gazed at her, her expression softened.

'Yet we must talk in private, you and I – and there's little privacy at Farthingdown. So...' she raised her eyebrows. 'In the absence of a fire to warm ourselves by, may I share your bed for a while?'

Without a word Revill got up, took the candle from her and placed it on the chest by the wall. He waited while she climbed under the covers and moved across to the far side of the bed. Then he took two of the three pillows and placed them behind her head, and having made her comfortable, got in beside her.

'You are thoughtful, sir,' the lady said approvingly; he was unsure in the dim light, but he believed she even smiled. 'Especially for a soldier, as you say you were. Now, perhaps you'll enlighten me further – for I'm quite sure of one thing: that you're no more a Surveyor of the Queen's Works than I am. So, shall we begin?'

NINE

It was a night to remember, Revill would think later, but not for any moment of passion. It was one of confession, for a decision occurred that in the end would bring him a measure of relief: he would throw caution aside, he decided, and tell Lady Gisela the unvarnished truth. It had become too heavy a burden, and it must be shed.

And so, he did: the whole tale, from the wet morning at the Artillery Yard in Shoreditch when he had been summoned to Walsingham's house by Sir Thomas Heneage, to the bloody encounter that day with Turnbull's hired men in the stables at Weybridge. By the time he had finished he was on his feet, wrapped in a coverlet against the chill, speaking of his shame at agreeing to Heneage's brutal mission – and of his resolve, already made, that he could not carry it out. Thereafter, feeling spent, he slumped down on the bed and fell silent.

'By heaven... you poor fellow,' Lady Gisela said, after what seemed an eternity.

He looked up sharply.

'And what a rogue he is,' she added, her voice rising. 'Not a thought for anyone but himself... greedy and unprincipled, unfit for proper society... to think he was once a handsome young blade, who had the girls flocking about him.'

'You mean Sir Thomas Heneage, my lady?' Revill enquired. 'I thought-'

A RELUCTANT ASSASSIN

'No - I mean my son!'

She cut him short, gripping the edge of the bedsheet. 'I knew there was something dark behind it all,' she went on, seemingly piecing it out as she spoke. 'Norris – whose name isn't even Norris, you tell me – never truly cared for Charis. I saw it, as did others – only Sir Abel was so beguiled by the man and his tales, he wouldn't listen. And the poor girl was so smitten, I never found the occasion to confront her. But now...' she shivered.

'I knew Hugh had sunk into baseness,' she went on. 'I heard report of it, from men who knew and tried to warn me. Yet I never thought he would play such a cruel trick on his sister - though he tormented her often enough when they were children. When I think what a sham wedding would have done to her, once the truth was known – not to say what it would have done to Sir Abel. It could have killed him!'

She let out a breath, gazing at Revill. Neither of them needed to reflect that Heneage's orders to him had been designed to bring about that very outcome.

'I am undone, sir,' she said at last, in a sorrowful voice. 'You have undone me.'

'And if I could call these past days back and choose another path, I would do so,' he said, with an effort. 'At supper you named Aubridge a coward – yet it's I who should wear that badge. My shame is complete.'

'No.' Suddenly, Lady Gisela startled him by putting out a hand and laying it upon his. 'Your love for your sister ruled you – you were entrapped. It was a vicious ploy by Heneage. Believe me when I say I bear no ill-will towards you – especially since you found that you could not do the deed. You've been kind to my husband...' she gave a little cough, that was almost a laugh. 'You even saved his life – hardly the mark of an assassin.'

Having no reply to make, he gave a shake of his head. They were silent for a while, each busy with their own thoughts. Then:

'You must make things right with your servant,' the lady said, quite firmly. 'Or, should I say your sergeant. It seems to me he's as loyal as they come.' And when he barely nodded: 'Afterwards, when you feel strong enough, you must leave here quietly. I will manage Sir Abel...' she paused, gathering her resolve. 'Indeed, we will manage it together... all of us at Farthingdown. The suit against Cowley will be dropped of course, as will the wild notion of our hosting the Queen.' She gave an impatient sigh. 'I said to you before, in the gardens that morning, that I could not compass who put the notion into the heads of Her Majesty's councillors. It seemed preposterous to everyone except Sir Abel, who was so eager to believe it that it clouded his judgement. Now that I understand, I bitterly despise Heneage for his wicked and tawdry scheme.'

'As do I, madam,' Revill said. 'Yet when all's said and sifted, I'm but a soldier - a captain of artillery, who deals death by battery of cannon. He chose me not for those skills I possess, but for my weakness: my sweet-natured sister, whom I would never see harmed. I could not live with myself...' he sighed. 'And that burr yet remains. I see no solution, save the one I touched upon: to warn her and her husband to flee this country, and start life anew.'

'I would help you if I could,' Lady Gisela said, after a moment. 'Yet no course comes to mind. Perhaps, when you leave us, you should ride to your kinfolk in Devon before returning to London. I could spin a tale about your needing to rest here a few more days – I mean, after that unfortunate fall from your horse.'

Their eyes met - and despite everything, he found himself comforted. There was a kindness in the Mistress

A RELUCTANT ASSASSIN

of Farthingdown, and a strength that he had sensed from the beginning. He had small doubt that she would carry out her resolve: to calm Sir Abel and make him see reason. But another thought occurred, which he decided to voice.

'What of your son, my lady?'

'Him?' Her mouth tightened. 'He has lost - lost everything. I will tell Sir Abel, sparing his feelings, that Hugh intends to remain abroad on the Queen's service. Meanwhile I will try to get a message to him that he should not return to Farthingdown... I may say there's danger to his life. Though even that may not keep him away, for he still expects to inherit.' She gave a sigh. 'After what transpired between you and Master Norris – or Turnbull, if you will – I doubt that he'll do as you bade him, when he next sees Hugh. More likely he will tell all – and hence, you'll have made another enemy.'

But to that, Revill gave a rueful smile. 'In truth, one more of those would make little difference to me,' he said.

A moment passed, before Lady Gisela sighed again and sat up straight.

'Well now: in spite of the grim aspect of the matter, you have soothed my mind a little,' she said. 'In the morning I'll be your hostess again, and we will keep our distance while you recover from your wound. This discourse shall be our secret.'

But when their eyes met again, she hesitated. 'Were I twenty years younger, sir, and we were elsewhere,' she added, 'the outcome might have been quite different. Now, will you help me up? The light burns low, and I fear to fall in the dark.'

With a nod Revill rose, turned back the covers and drew her from the bed. But before releasing her hand, he bent and kissed it.

'It was a night I will cherish,' he murmured.

JOHN PILKINGTON

Then he sat down as she took up the candle and went from the room, leaving him once again in darkness.

***

Saturday dawned, and he slept heavily. When he finally awoke, stiff and sore from his wound, the autumn sun was up, and someone had already been in his room to leave a bowl of water and a ball of plain soap. Rising and moving to the window, he peered out and saw the old gardener at work. The house was very quiet, he thought – whereupon the memory of his night-time conversation with Lady Gisela sprang up.

It stayed with him as he inspected his wound, which mercifully seemed not to be infected, and as he dressed. He thought then of Sir Abel's collapse, his bitter words; he saw Ashman, earnestly entreating his mistress to take over Farthingdown – and then he stiffened. Now he saw Tom Bright standing in the rain outside the barber-surgeon's house, telling him he would stay with the horses. He must speak with him – and soon.

He took breakfast alone, but hardly ate anything; Lady Gisela was in her private closet, he was told, and Sir Abel still abed. His physician had been summoned from Weybridge and was with him already. This much he learned from Mab, when he went to the kitchens to ask the whereabouts of his sergeant. But the maid had not seen him since early that morning. She was subdued, he thought, as were the other servants, some of whom gave him sidelong glances; what had occurred at supper the previous night would doubtless be known throughout Farthingdown. Now resolved to take his leave as soon as he could, he went out to the stables.

On entering, he found the young stable-lad who, two days earlier, had pointed him to the hut where he had encountered a drunken Ashman. There was no sign of Tom

A RELUCTANT ASSASSIN

Bright - or even his horse. But the boy was eager to please, his face lighting up in anticipation of a tip.

'Tom's out in the paddock, sir,' he volunteered. 'He was up early, exercising Malachi for you. Now he's taken the jennet.'

Revill glanced over to his horse, saw that he appeared contented – then gave a start.

'Are you certain he's only exercising the mount? He wasn't carrying a pack, or anything?' And when the boy looked puzzled, he added: 'What I mean is, did he say he would return?'

'Not in so many words, sir. And he didn't have any pack that I saw…'

He trailed off as his questioner turned away; the tip would have to wait.

Mercifully, any unease on Revill's part was misplaced. He walked briskly to the paddock, where three or four horses stood bunched in a corner and saw Bright walking his jennet on the far side of the field. Having hailed him, he climbed stiffly through the fence and started forward. After a moment the little sergeant dismounted, turned the animal loose and waited for him to approach.

'I thought you might have left,' Revill said, with a wry look. 'And God knows, I'd hardly blame you if you had.'

'How's the wound, Captain?' Bright asked, after a moment.

'It's mending,' Revill told him. He paused, then: 'You'll have heard about Sir Abel, and his taking ill at supper?'

'The whole manor knows of it. Seems it's happened before, only not so bad. But…' He hesitated, then: 'I heard something else too. Lady Gisela left her chamber in the night, told her maidservant she was going to sit up with Sir Abel for a while. Only, his body-servant was watching him all the time in case he had another turn. So, nobody's sure where the lady went.' He raised an eyebrow. 'Bit cold for wandering about the house, wouldn't you say?'

'Shall we take a walk, Tom?' Revill said without expression. 'There are things that need to be aired.'

After a moment, the other nodded.

They walked in silence back to the manor, through the gardens and out past the trees to the meadow that sloped down to the lake. Here they were alone, out of sight of the house and its occupants. Finally, they stopped near the edge of the water, where a breeze ruffled its surface. But when Revill turned to face his companion, Bright was ready for him.

'You could have told me, from the very first,' he said, somewhat grimly.

'I know it...' Revill looked aside briefly. 'I wasn't thinking straight.'

'How did they lime you?' The other asked. 'For there must have been some powerful persuasion, to set you to it... was it Jenna they threatened?'

'No.' He shook his head. 'My sister Katherine.'

'What – she who married the papist?' Bright broke in. 'By the Christ.'

Revill sat down heavily on the grass, looking out across the tranquil lake. Sitting down beside him, his sergeant waited for him to begin. And thereafter, in a short time, he learned all he needed to know about Sir Thomas Heneage's orders, and the sham inspection on behalf of the Queen's Surveyor of Works. As to what had followed since their arrival at Farthingdown: Bright knew enough, and could piece out the rest.

'What a whoreson rogue is our Vice-Chamberlain,' he said, when his captain had finished. 'Mayhap someone should arrange a little accident for him, instead.'

A RELUCTANT ASSASSIN

Revill said nothing.

'But it was a fool's errand,' the sergeant went on. 'I know you'd never have killed Sir Abel. He's to be pitied, him and his whole household - even that sour-faced steward.'

'There's more to it, Tom,' Revill said, turning to him. And he found himself speaking of Hugh Stanbury, his relations with the false suitor Turnbull, and the plan to sell Farthingdown. In the end, it was a relief to unburden himself – and an even greater relief that Bright seemed not to hold a grudge against him, now that the truth was out.

'And you're right: I should have laid it all forth, before we even left London,' Revill added. 'I'd no business dragging you into it.'

'Jesus, Captain… what a maelstrom.' Bright plucked a tuft of grass and threw it idly aside. 'But you're surely correct that you weren't thinking straight. If the deed had to be done, you could have hired a couple of varlets like Turnbull did, and sent them down here to do it-'

'And if I had?' Revill broke in. 'Now that you see how the land lies - what kind of man Sir Abel is - do you think I could have lived with what I'd done?'

'Not easily,' came the reply. 'But you'd have weathered it, in time. It was for your sister…' he lowered his gaze. 'Besides, if any of us were to dwell too long on what we saw and did in the Low Countries, we'd all end up in Bedlam. More, mayhap we should count ourselves lucky we weren't at Sluis, or Zutphen.'

They were silent then, for their memories were the same. But for Revill, one chilling fact stood out: since he had failed to obey Heneage's order to kill Sir Abel, how long might it be before someone else was sent to carry it out?

Finally, the sergeant drew a breath and looked up. 'So, Captain, what's to be done? Ride down to Devonshire and warn your sister?' He paused. 'Do you want me to go?'

'No - you should get back to London, and I'll pay you off,' Revill answered. 'Most men would have already done what I said, on the way here: left my company for good.'

'Yet, you know me better... or so I thought.'

'I did - I do. And I ask your pardon, from the depths of my soiled heart.'

'Oh, to the devil with that.'

Bright made a dismissive gesture. 'You'll come at a way out of this turmoil, Captain, as you always have. I know it, for I'm alive to bear witness.' He got to his feet, frowning at the damp patch on his breeches. 'Tomorrow's the sabbath - will you be fit to ride then? We can talk on the journey, see what comes up.'

With a nod, Revill too stood up, gazing absently across the riffled water. Tom Bright's mention of the war had stirred an odd notion in him: that he'd had no scruples in putting to death two hired ruffians the day before - likely ex-soldiers like himself, with nothing to sell but their fighting skills. And yet he had found himself in turmoil over the life of a half-mad nobleman who was such a danger to himself, he could suffer a fatal accident at any time. It seemed absurd... drawing in a breath of cool air, he turned to his sergeant.

'You'd best take your farewell of Mab,' he said.

Bright gave a sigh, and nodded.

***

For Revill, the rest of the day seemed to pass by so slowly, his spirits flagged with it. He saw nothing of Lady Gisela, and dined alone. Ashman too appeared to be avoiding him, he thought, and was busying himself with household matters. Sir Abel's physician, it transpired, had

A RELUCTANT ASSASSIN

departed leaving some powders, and instructions that his patient be allowed to rest. The whole manor, it seemed, wore an air of unease, like a cloak that might slip at any moment.

In the afternoon, feeling restless, he retired to his chamber and let it be known that he was completing his survey report; only Lady Gisela and Tom Bright, he guessed, would know that this was but a tale. Instead, he tried to compose a letter for Heneage, to be sent to Sir Francis Walsingham's house in Seething Lane. But he soon gave up: he would take a risk and confront the man in person, he decided. Perhaps there were some other service he might perform, to placate the Vice-Chamberlain - though the notion gave him little hope.

By evening, with little desire to go down to supper, he was seated by an open window, thinking of his return to Jenna on the morrow. He frowned, thinking of how he had spun her another tale to explain his absence; now, he was tired of lying. How she might deal with the truth of it, he was unsure... he gazed out for the last time over the Farthingdown gardens, growing dim as the dusk darkened to night. Tomorrow, he would be gone.

Growing drowsy, he was slumped in the chair when a commotion outside startled him into wakefulness. As he looked round, the door flew open, and Ashman hurried in with an air of agitation.

'Is something amiss...?' Revill began, but was cut short.

'It's Sir Abel.' The steward's face was pale in the half-light. 'He's gone!'

'Gone where? Wasn't someone with him?'

'He struck the man down,' Ashman said, in a voice of disbelief. 'His own body-servant - old Lawrence, who's been with him since boyhood!'

Seeing how shaken he was, Revill stood up and moved to calm him. 'Well, surely he cannot go far. Have you not ordered the servants to seek him?'

'You don't understand - he's left the house, and in a hurry,' Ashman snapped. 'He was seen making for the stables – and he hasn't ridden a horse in weeks. He might fall, or ...' he grimaced. 'He's not himself - we must do something!'

'Very well, Master Ashman: I will go.'

Raising a hand, Revill stayed him; here at last was something useful he could do. Telling the man to find Tom Bright, he was about to leave the chamber - then he paused and, on impulse, took his sword from the wall where it hung. He buckled it on as he walked out into the passage, his mind busy. From below, he was aware of voices raised. He descended the staircase to find Lady Gisela standing in the hallway – and seeing the look on her face, stopped in his tracks. Some of the Farthingdown servants stood about her in apparent alarm. But at sight of Revill, she took a hurried step towards him.

'Sir Abel is beside himself,' she said, her voice taut. 'He leaped from his bed, crying out he would be avenged... when his man tried to remonstrate, he was knocked aside. He came down in a rage, half-dressed – everyone shrank from him.'

'Ashman says he went to take horse,' Revill said, with a calm that was clearly lacking on all sides. 'Where would he go?'

The lady drew a breath and tried to match his composure. 'To John Cowley's farm,' she said, after a moment. 'Do you see? The matter of the will, and what Aubridge told you, has unnerved him - he cannot bear it. I think it has played upon him all night, and throughout the

A RELUCTANT ASSASSIN

day.' She gave a shudder. 'While I... I was not present, to comfort him.'

Their eyes met, but fleetingly.

'I'll stop him,' Revill said firmly – and forgetting himself, he placed his hands on her shoulders. 'He'll come to no harm. My horse is swift and sees in the dark like an owl.'

Footsteps sounded, and both of them turned to see Ashman coming heavily down the stairs. With barely a glance at the two of them he took charge of the servants, sending one to rouse Tom Bright. But the man had barely turned to obey when the sergeant himself appeared with clothing rumpled, his breeches half-laced. Revill took one glance and guessed he had been making the most of his last night with Mab.

'We must ride, Tom,' he said. 'Sir Abel's in danger.'

He turned quickly from Lady Gisela, and strode to the doors. Without a word, Bright followed. And but a few minutes later, under the bewildered gazes of the stablemen, they had got themselves horsed and were already passing through the gates of Farthingdown on to the lane that led south: towards the farm of John Cowley, Sir Abel's neighbour and opponent in a disastrous suit of law.

Privately, Revill could only hope that they were not too late.

TEN

The distance was short, and they rode with care lest the horses should stumble in the dark. For Revill, the memory arose of his encounter in the field with Cowley some days before, and their harsh exchange. With what he now knew, the turnabout was stark: he found himself as uneasy for the safety of Sir Abel's neighbour as he was for the old knight himself.

This much he had gleaned from the stable-lad, his trusted informant: that the Master of Farthingdown had arrived in a sweat, his fur-trimmed gown thrown over his night clothes, railed at everyone and ordered his old hunting-horse saddled at speed. He wasn't even wearing boots, but a pair of broidered slippers. Too chastened to reason with him, the stablemen had obeyed, then watched him dig heels into his mount and ride off in a fury. Yet, knowing him as they did, perhaps such behaviour had not surprised them unduly... such were the thoughts that flew through Revill's mind as he rode, until his sergeant diverted him. Having had only a cursory explanation of the matter, Bright was both puzzled and wary.

'What in God's name will he do, Captain?' He asked, easing his jennet close to Malachi. 'I know he's cracked as a walnut, but he can't be bent on murder... can he?'

'I don't know,' Revill answered. 'In truth, I doubt if he even knows himself.'

A RELUCTANT ASSASSIN

'I've heard gossip about the will, and how he hates farmer Cowley,' the sergeant said. 'Only, I thought after you saw the lawyer in Weybridge... or is there more?'

'If there is, I don't care,' Revill told him. 'Just now it's Lady Gisela I'm thinking of.'

His sergeant fell silent. And soon, a glow appeared ahead of them. Slowing the horses, they saw a gateway and, beyond that, the bulk of a large farmhouse where lights showed at the downstairs windows. As they clattered into the yard, a door opened somewhere, and a voice cried out in alarm.

'Here's another of them! Sweet God, save us...'

It was drowned by the barking of a dog, which came hurtling out of the doorway. Quickly Revill and Bright drew rein, peering into the gloom. The horses shied as the dog yapped and frisked about them, until Revill bent low in the saddle and spoke. To his relief it recognised him and ceased barking. Lifting his head, he looked towards the house and saw a figure in the doorway, silhouetted against the light.

'Be easy – we mean no harm!' He called. He dismounted quickly, as did his sergeant, and stepped forward. 'I seek Sir Abel Stanbury–'

He broke off as a whinnying sounded from a few yards away. Looking round, he glimpsed what must be Sir Abel's horse, its reins dangling loosely, stamping nervously on the cobbles. The dog trotted about its legs, then yelped as the horse kicked out.

'You seek him? Then by heaven, sir – you could be our saviour!'

The person in the doorway spoke up again, in agitation. And when Revill and Bright drew near, they found a slim girl of thirteen or fourteen years, clad in a plain frock. Seeing them loom up out of the darkness, she drew back.

'Is John Cowley your father, mistress?' Revill asked. 'Is he nearby?'

The girl nodded, clutching at the neck of her dress. 'We're in turmoil - it's like a demon has come here! Mother's locked my sisters and brothers up for safety...'

She broke off, gazing at the two of them in alarm, and Revill understood: to her they would look like the soldiers they had always been - armed and threatening.

'I promise you we've come to help,' he said, raising his hands in a calming gesture. 'I'm a guest of Sir Abel – he's unwell, and we're here to bring him home.'

'Is it so, sir?' The Cowley girl's expression changed. 'Then I pray you, hurry!'

With that she stepped inside, allowing the two of them to enter the house. As they did so, there were cries from above: the frightened squeals of children. Revill found himself in a large, plainly-furnished room, with a stairway nearby.

'What's your name, child?'

Bright spoke gently to the girl, trying to put her at ease. While Revill moved across the room towards a closed door at the rear, his sergeant remained by the stairs. From the floor above, noises continued.

'I'm Margaret,' came the shaky reply. 'I was with Mother when he burst in... you must aid her!'

'We will,' Bright said. 'Where's your father now – and is Sir Abel with him?'

Before she could answer, however, there came a dull thud from somewhere. Bright looked round to see Revill tense, his hand on his sword-hilt.

'In there,' he called out, nodding towards the rear door.

'What's through there?' Bright asked of Margaret. 'Where does it lead?'

A RELUCTANT ASSASSIN

'To Father's store, and his counting-room. Mother never goes in, as a rule...' she faltered, close to tears. 'I fear something terrible will happen!'

'What – you mean both your mother and father are in that room?'

The girl merely nodded, whereupon the sergeant moved to join Revill, whose hand was already on the latch. But when he tried it, the door would not yield.

'Someone's locked it.' He turned to Bright; now both of them could hear raised voices, and what sounded like a scuffle.

'You'd better stand back, Captain,' the sergeant said grimly. 'You don't want to tear your wound open.'

So, Revill moved aside as, with gritted teeth, Bright threw his shoulder violently against the door. With a crash of splintering wood, it gave way, allowing him to thrust it wide open. The two of them piled in... to stop dead.

Sir Abel Stanbury, clad only in his night-shirt, stood in the middle of a very small room, red-faced with anger – and holding an ancient, jewelled dagger. Facing him was John Cowley, unarmed and in shirt sleeves, fists raised to ward him off. At one side a stool and a small table had been overturned, spilling papers and other debris across the floor, while from a low beam a lantern swung dangerously. But what struck Revill and Bright most forcefully was the sight of a stout woman who must be the farmer's wife, wielding a heavy wooden ladle. Breathlessly, she turned about as the two men broke in, as did her husband - then:

'Get out, damn you!'

Sir Abel, hoarse with rage, flung a hand out at his would-be rescuers. As Revill eyed him, the old knight levelled his dagger. He was beyond reason: Revill saw the look, one he had seen on the faces of a hundred men-at-war, and caught his breath.

'You may die this night!' Sir Abel cried. 'You, and your damned lackey!' This with a baleful glare at Bright. 'I'll have my will – I'll avenge my poor father...'

On a sudden he broke off, turning by instinct – but he was too late. Mistress Cowley had swung the ladle with all her might and cracked him on the side of the head. And as her victim reeled, John Cowley at last found his voice.

'By the Christ, can't you stop him before he has a seizure?' He cried, his gaze shifting to Revill. 'He's Bedlam mad! He'll not rest until he's drawn blood!'

Revill's eyes flew from Cowley to his wild-eyed nemesis, swaying where he stood, blood starting to trickle down his cheek. Beside him he sensed Bright ready to spring, but put out a hand to stay him.

'Take her out of here,' he breathed, with a jerk of his head towards Mistress Cowley, who was gripping her weapon as if to deal another blow. 'Let her go to her children.'

The sergeant darted forward to seize the woman's arm. And when she gasped and struggled, he forced her hand down...

Whereupon matters went badly awry.

With a shriek, Mistress Cowley lashed out with her free hand and caught Bright full in the face – particularly his eye. With a hiss of pain, he loosened his grip – which allowed her to drop the ladle and begin beating him on the chest with her fists. For a second the men were dumbfounded, until John Cowley found his voice.

'Grace – stop! They're trying to help us!'

'I won't!' His wife cried. 'Not while that devil's on his feet!'

A RELUCTANT ASSASSIN

She meant Sir Abel, who still looked dazed from the blow she had dealt him. For a moment it appeared that he would sag – until Revill saw and reacted. Just in time, he managed to grip the man's wrist as he lunged forward with the poniard, prompting him to cry out. To his relief, Cowley seized the moment and grasped the other arm. In a trice the old knight was caught and pinioned, the three of them locked in a bizarre tableau: Revill grim and silent, Cowley panting, while the Master of Farthingdown...

Sir Abel started trembling violently. Struggling, mumbled words coming from his lips, he tugged this way and that between both his captors, before letting go of his dagger... but as it fell, his gaze fell with it. In a kind of daze, he watched it land on the rough floorboards... then he gave a shudder, his body quivering.

As the two let go of him in alarm, he slumped to the floor, twitched again... and was still.

Breathing hard, Revill stepped back. So did Cowley, his face haggard... while his wife fell against the wall with a whimper, her hand going to her mouth.

Tom Bright, a hand pressed to one eye, took a pace away from the woman. 'Captain?' He began... but stopped himself, looking down at the still form, lying motionless.

There was silence, until Revill knelt to put a hand to Sir Abel's neck, felt the great artery, then stood up slowly. The others stared downwards, speechless.

'Go and comfort your children,' he said roughly, turning to the farmer's wife. 'Tell them there's naught to fear now.'

She hesitated, her gaze going to her husband, who managed a nod.

'Keep them upstairs,' he said. And when at last she obeyed, hurrying out with what sounded like a sob, his eyes returned to his slain assailant.

'By heaven... now I've gone and killed him,' he stammered. 'The blasted old fool...'

'No.'

Somewhat harshly, Revill cut him short. 'You no more killed him than I did - indeed, you're even less to blame.' And as the notion struck him with full force, he let out a long breath. He looked at Bright, who had lowered his hand to reveal a face streaked with blood.

'It's true,' the sergeant muttered. 'I'd say it's a miracle he lived as long as he did...' his gaze went from Cowley to his captain, and back to Cowley. 'You didn't seek this fight. You were unarmed... you were protecting your family.'

But now that the storm had passed, the farmer was aghast. Barely aware of what he did, he caught up the stool from the floor and sat down heavily. 'My God, what'll happen now?' He said, looking up at Revill. 'Will I be arrested? He's – he was a nobleman...'

'He was unwell,' Revill said, meeting his eye. 'Everyone knew it. You spoke of a seizure, and that's what I'll report. He came here in a rage, not in his senses – he threatened you with a dagger, and you tried to reason with him. All of that's true, is it not?'

'But what about Grace?' Cowley asked weakly. 'She might have split his skull...' On a sudden, his face screwed up as if in pain. 'Will they take her too? I couldn't bear it!'

'No-one will take her – nor you, either. You have my word.'

Calmer now, Revill drew closer to the man and laid a hand on his shoulder. 'You must trust me to manage this, along with the Farthingdown people. They will help, I believe...' he turned to Bright.

A RELUCTANT ASSASSIN

'Will you stay here, Tom? I'll ride to Lady Gisela and break the news, then bring back men to take up the body.' He frowned. 'Someone needs to look at your eye…'

'We'll attend to that – it's the very least we should do.'

It was Cowley who spoke, struggling to master himself. Getting slowly to his feet, he nodded at Bright. 'I pray you, come to the kitchen. My daughter Margaret is skilled enough… though not so skilled as Grace,' he added. 'But she should stay where she is… are you content to trust us?'

'I might be,' the sergeant said, after a moment. He looked at Revill, who nodded.

And so, averting their eyes from the body, the two men made their way out through the ruined doorway. Cowley followed, the three of them crossing the main room to pause at the foot of the stairs. Above them, all seemed quiet – whereupon Margaret hurried out from somewhere, her face filled with anguish. At sight of her father, she let out a cry.

'It's over, lambkin,' he muttered. 'I promise.' Then he staggered as the girl threw her arms about him, bursting into tears.

Bright threw Revill a look that told him he shouldn't delay. Whereupon, without further word he left the house, stepping out into the night air. In the yard the horses milled about anxiously, and Cowley's dog ran past him through the doorway. From indoors, voices sounded, low and subdued.

Breathing deeply, he went to Malachi, placed a soothing hand on his neck, then caught up the reins. And a moment later, he was riding back through the gateway and into the lane, his heart as heavy as a cannonball.

***

Lady Gisela, seated on a chair in the marigold room, received the news with remarkable calm; Leonard Ashman, however, looked aghast.

'Dead - from a seizure?' He stared at Revill. 'Are you certain?'

With a nod, Revill lowered his eyes.

'But... what caused it? Did he and Cowley dispute? Was there some brabble, or-'

'Leonard, I pray you.'

The steward blinked, turning to face Her Ladyship. 'I trust that Master Revill will acquaint us with the facts, as soon as he may,' she went on. 'Just now, there are things to be done... will you call the servants together?'

After a moment, Ashman nodded and got to his feet, his brow creased as if in pain. When he moved to the door, Revill would have followed, but the lady stayed him.

'Will you tarry, please?' She indicated a chair facing hers. Alone with her, Revill sat down.

'I need you to answer one question first,' she said, drawing a breath. 'Then I will ask you to swear to it.' And when he gave a nod, she eyed him and asked: 'Did you kill him?'

'To the best of my knowledge, no,' he answered. 'But swear to it entirely, I fear I cannot.'

Lady Gisela remained silent.

'And nor did John Cowley kill him,' he added. 'In truth, I suspect only a physician could know the real cause of it. Your pardon, but...' he drew a breath. 'It's my belief that Sir Abel brought about his own death. If you wish me to recount all that happened, I will.'

'Well then, I do,' came the reply.

And so, he told her - and quite soon, it felt almost like a continuation of their candlelit conversation in his chamber, only the night before. He told her everything –

A RELUCTANT ASSASSIN

apart from one fact which he decided to omit: the blow to the head Grace Cowley had given Sir Abel. In his heart, he believed that the Cowley family's troubles just now were grave enough.

Lady Gisela listened in utter silence - until at last, as Revill spoke of Sir Abel's fall, she raised a hand abruptly.

'I pray you, cease now.'

He stopped and lowered his eyes. But after a while, when she had made no sound, he looked up to see a tear coursing down her cheek.

'I'm most heartily sorry, my lady,' was all he could say. 'And moreover, whether your husband died because his heart stopped, or from some sudden flux to the head, or…' he sighed. 'I will hold myself to blame - always. For it was I who brought grief upon you both – indeed, upon your whole family by one means or another.'

A pause followed, then: 'In a way you did – you, and Her Majesty's Vice-Chamberlain,' she said. 'And now you may return to him to report your commission carried out as instructed – and hence, I suppose your sister will be safe.'

He looked sharply at her, as she drew a lace kerchief from her sleeve.

'But then, you and I will always know that it's but a part of the tale,' she added, dabbing at her cheek. 'Sir Abel's sickness, which he bore for almost the whole of his life, most stoically… his delusions about the will, and monies due to him, let alone his notion of the Queen's visiting Farthingdown. Indeed, some might even say that it was the truth that killed him once he was made to face it.'

Revill made no reply.

'And now I shall grieve, as a widow must,' the lady said with a sigh. 'But in my heart, I will be thankful – for he is at peace and can have the ease he longed for.'

'What would you have me do, madam?' He asked, finding his voice at last. 'You've only to name it. If you wish, I'll leave at once...'

'What, tonight?' Lady Gisela raised her eyebrows. 'Somewhat late for a ride back to London, is it not - and with your servant still at the farm?' To his surprise, her expression softened. 'Nay... you need to rest. I haven't forgotten your injury, even if you had.'

Her gaze strayed briefly towards his shoulder – whereupon he turned quickly and saw that the sleeve of his doublet was soaked with blood. In the tussle at the farm, he had torn the stitches without even knowing – and almost at once felt a surge of pain, as if his body had only now given him permission to feel it.

'I'll accept your hospitality for one more night,' he said, getting slowly to his feet. 'Now I must return to Cowley...' he hesitated, then: 'He is broken by what occurred, my lady. He too blames himself, though he was not at fault - I pray you will remember that, when the officers of law begin their enquiries.'

To his relief, the lady gave a nod. 'Now that all's been laid bare – the question of the lawsuit, I mean...' she sighed again. 'I think everyone will hope that the inquest be brief, and no-one held to blame. I will call upon such friends as I have – and on Aubridge too. Perhaps you can write a deposition before you leave, and Ashman can witness it?'

'Of course,' Revill nodded. On a sudden he was restless to busy himself; what feelings may come later, he would not dwell on. Yet he paused and took a step towards Lady Gisela.

'One thing I do swear,' he said. 'That Sir Abel will always be in my heart, for his friendship and for the good

A RELUCTANT ASSASSIN

man he tried to be. He did not deserve to suffer so... and nor did you.'

She met his eye briefly, without reply. But when he made his bow and began to turn away, she lifted a hand, palm downwards.

Bending low, he kissed it and left her.

***

Late that night – long past midnight, when all that could be done had been done – he fell exhaustedly across his bed. But though his eyes closed his mind was active, the pictures flitting by in stark clarity. He saw again the yard of Cowley's farm as he, Ashman and four of the Farthingdown menservants rode in, with a low cart bringing up the rear. He saw the milling of horses – and Sir Abel's mount, now unsaddled, with one of the farmer's young sons attending it. And there was Cowley himself, muffled in the shepherd's cape he had worn when Revill had first encountered him. There were voices, soft and strained, as Ashman spoke with the man before issuing orders to his servants. And finally, after Tom Bright had come outside to join Revill, a bandage across one side of his face, there followed the saddest sight of all: the body of the old knight, shrouded and covered with his fur-trimmed gown, being carried out by his servants to be laid on the cart. The two men watched in silence as Sir Abel's horse was brought up and tied to the rear. Then the driver was seated and shaking the reins, and the little cavalcade passed out through the gates, the servants riding behind. With bowed head John Cowley watched them depart, then walked back into the house.

Only Ashman, Revill and Bright had remained – whereupon, somewhat to their embarrassment, the steward made a choking sound. Standing by his horse, reins in hand, he began to weep.

'I knew he would not live much longer,' he murmured, eyes on the cobbles at his feet. 'Every time he was unmanned, every time he looked as if he would shake himself to death, I feared it - we all did. My mistress...' he shook his head. 'She is the bravest and finest woman I ever knew – she sacrificed everything for him. The life she could have had... the suitors who importuned her father, who in his pride would have only a nobleman of ancient lineage for her spouse...'

He looked up fiercely, his face wet with tears. 'She was my Aurora... my Astraea! Yet no-one knew, let alone my lady herself. I adored her, from the first day she came as a bride – and I do still!'

His face taut with loss, shame and feelings only he understood, Ashman gazed at Revill. Beside him, Tom Bright looked away. But Revill took a pace towards the grief-stricken man and touched his arm briefly.

'I see that,' he said. 'And I suspect she always has, too. Now, will you ride back with us, and offer her what comfort you can? I believe she will be glad of it.'

A moment had passed then, before the steward had given a nod. It was the last image Revill recalled, before he fell into an exhausted sleep.

ELEVEN

They left Farthingdown on the morning of the next day: the sabbath, and exactly one week since Revill had stood in the rain at the Artillery Yard in Shoreditch, drilling his bedraggled trained band and oblivious to what was about to befall him.

That afternoon, he had learned, the household would hold a service with Lady Gisela as the principal mourner. The body of Sir Abel had been laid out in a room at the rear of the manor, surrounded by candles. Arrangements were being made for the knight's funeral, and word had already been sent to his son and daughter. Revill had agreed to pause in Weybridge on his homeward journey to hand Thomas Aubridge a letter from the widow, and to request him to call upon the coroner. Naturally, an inquest would follow.

He rode stiffly, holding his arm across his chest. His wound had been heavily bandaged by Mab, whose face early that morning was stained with tears. Indeed, now that Sir Abel's body was brought home, all the servants had given way to a grief that was both unfeigned and heartfelt. The manor was in mourning and would remain so for months. Mab's feelings, however, were compounded by the departure of Tom Bright; in the end, their parting had been more sorrowful than the sergeant would admit. He now rode in silence beside his captain, a new bandage over one eye. The two of them looked like soldiers returning from battle; to Revill, the analogy was apt enough.

Under his coat he wore a fresh shirt and a doublet given to him by Ashman, who was making a strong effort to take the reins at Farthingdown; his farewell to Revill had been formal and a little embarrassed, before he had hurried off to his tasks. Lady Gisela had not been seen since the previous night, but remained in her chamber. Meanwhile tidings were going out - and yet, in the silence that lay over the manor, there was an air of calm. Rumours were rife, but one matter brought unspoken relief: there would be no more talk of lawsuits. Though the future was uncertain, it seemed that at least, there would be one.

Having passed the short journey without speaking, the two men entered Weybridge uneasily; the memory of the bloody encounter in the stable made them tense and watchful. When Revill said he would stop at the lawyer's home only to deliver his tidings, Bright said he would wait beside the bridge. And so, they parted, the sergeant easing his mount into a trot; passers-by glanced at both men, but thankfully gave no sign of recognition. Revill rode briskly to Aubridge's, dismounted before the house and let Malachi's reins dangle, expecting to be out again in minutes.

The man of law, however, had other ideas.

To begin with he insisted on Revill staying while he read Lady Gisela's letter – and then read it again, his brow creasing by degrees until he was almost scowling. Finally, he looked up and gave a long sigh.

'God in heaven,' he puffed. 'I don't know whether to weep, or to leap for joy.'

Standing before him in his cluttered parlour, Revill stiffened.

A RELUCTANT ASSASSIN

'I mean...' Aubridge gave a cough and made an effort to look contrite. 'I'm pierced to the heart – of course I am. I knew Sir Abel most of my life - and I've talked him out of more rash decisions than you can imagine, sir.' This, with a frosty look at Revill. 'Only, with what's occurred...' he broke off with a frown. 'I'm surprised that Lady Gisela asked you to convey the sad news. Are you privy to the circumstances of Sir Abel's demise? In truth, I thought you'd have left Farthingdown long since... do you care to enlighten me?'

But Revill had no desire for conversation. Instead, he spoke briefly of Sir Abel's fall into madness, and a violent seizure that had followed. 'In time, you may learn more from Lady Gisela and her steward,' he finished. 'And the inquest, when it takes place.'

'Ah, yes... the inquest.' Aubridge pondered her matter. 'That will be an important event - and it could be that, as a witness to Sir Abel's behaviour of late, you will be called to appear yourself.'

In fact, that possibility had already occurred to Revill, who knew how these matters generally played out – and he had no desire to be available to testify. Upon which, a notion occurred to him with some force: that when all things were considered, England was no place for him now. Better to take himself abroad again, even to fight; the reality fell upon him like a dead weight. And yet, there was Jenna to think of...

'Do you hear me, sir?'

Aubridge's sharp question broke his thoughts. Drawing a breath, he nodded.

'I do - and whatever I can recall concerning Sir Abel, I'll keep to myself for the present. I've conveyed the tidings, and now I'll take my leave.'

'Very well, but...' the lawyer coughed again. 'Can you tell me how the land lies, just now, at Farthingdown? I mean, has the son and heir been informed, not to mention Lady-'

'Lady Charis?' Revill broke in, raising his eyebrows. 'I understand that word has been sent. But just now, shouldn't your task be to make haste to the manor yourself, and offer your services to the widow? Or do you think only of what gains you may come at yourself?'

'Eh?' Aubridge blinked, before one of his scowls appeared. 'How dare you address me in that manner! And now I think upon it - as I once said - I'm still uncertain as to why you ever journeyed to Farthingdown. To be plain, Revill, I do not trust you!'

'Nor I you, sir,' Revill replied mildly. 'But I believe I'll live with it.'

He turned to go, then paused. 'Though what I'll say to you is this: that the truth about Sir Abel's lawsuit, and the hopelessness of his case, was made plain to him before he died. It was a sore blow to him – as no doubt was the realisation that you'd never found the courage to tell him. Some might even say that the knowledge of it played a part in his final and fatal madness - but time will tell. That, and the findings of the inquest jury.'

Whereupon he turned away, even as the other leaped up from his chair – so abruptly that it fell back against a wall of shelves. As he reached the door, Revill caught sight of dusty scrolls, tied with ribbons and tagged with seals, tumbling to the floor around Master Aubridge. The last thing he saw was the lawyer's horror-stricken face, before he opened the door and strode outside.

A minute later he was in the saddle, urging Malachi from a trot to a canter as he left Weybridge behind; he did not look back.

A RELUCTANT ASSASSIN
***

The day was damp and cloudy, but mercifully there was no rain. Revill and Bright rode steadily through the little Surrey towns, reversing their journey of a week before, stopping only to water the horses. By the time they came to Newington, dusk was falling and both men were tired and hungry. Yet it was a relief to reach Southwark, and to see the lights of London across the Thames. They were just in time, for the Bridge Gate was about to close, and they were among the last travellers to enter the city. Finally, at the junction of New Fish Street and Thames Street, they reined in with the hum of the great town about them, the horses' breath clouding in the cool air.

'Here's where I leave you, Captain,' Bright said, turning to face him.

'Not for too long, I hope?' Revill enquired, meeting his unbandaged eye.

'Depends.' The sergeant said, squinting at him. Whereupon his captain reached inside his coat, drew out the purse he had prepared and handed it to him. As he took it, Bright felt its weight and showed his surprise.

'Feels generous. Blood money, is it?'

But he nodded his thanks - and now there was little to say. Briefly they clasped hands, leaning from their saddles, before turning their mounts away from one another.

'If you need me to watch your trained band blundering about, you know where to find me,' the sergeant said, raising his voice. 'But not yet, eh? I mean to get drunk for a week.'

And then he was gone, riding west along Stockfishmonger Row towards his lodgings in Dowgate. Revill watched him disappear, his heart heavier than he would have admitted. But he drew a breath, shook the reins and urged Malachi northwards up Fish Street Hill. At the crossing with East Cheap, with its scattering of beggars, he too turned westward as far as Candlewick Street before arriving at last in Abchurch Lane: his lodging for almost a year now, since he and Jenna had made home together.

The street was quiet when he dismounted and led the horse to his usual stable; the place was home to Malachi, who needed food and rest. Revill left him with the ostler, walked the short distance to the house and halted. No light showed at the window, but finding the door unlocked he entered. In the narrow hallway he paused until the rear door flew open, spilling light out - and there she stood, in the same sea-green frock she had worn on the day he left.

'By St Piran…' at sight of him, she sagged. 'You put the fear of God into me.'

'Expecting someone else, were you?' He enquired wryly. But when she hurried forward, he folded his arms about her. After a moment, she drew back to peer at him.

'In truth, I almost did – expect another,' she said. 'I'm mighty relieved it's you.'

He returned her gaze, thinking she looked tired and somewhat strained - then he grunted in pain. In alarm, she let go of him.

'What - more battle-wounds?' Her face clouded. 'Don't tell me it was another fencing accident.'

'Not exactly…' he tried a smile, but it barely worked; on a sudden, he felt as if he could sleep where he stood. Jenna's frown changed to a look of concern.

'Come, seat yourself,' she said. 'There's ale, and a fish pie from the bakehouse. It's cold, but I expect it'll serve.'

She turned quickly to enter the kitchen. Revill followed her, finding his mind eased by the familiar surroundings and then, as he removed his coat and sword and put them aside, by the sight of his auburn-haired Cornish lover bustling about. He sank down at the table where a pile of

A RELUCTANT ASSASSIN

tailored sleeves and stomachers lay, waiting to be broidered with silk; Jenna's skills were always in demand. Soon a mug of ale appeared, which he took up thirstily and drained in one. He lowered it, feeling the heavy liquid fill his stomach, and let out a long sigh.

'It looks to me as if you've another tale to tell,' Jenna said.

She brought a platter over and set it nearby. He met her enquiring gaze, then looked down at the wedge of pie and the hunk of rye bread. But in his mind images began to swirl about, along with a murmur of voices: Ashman's, Sir Abel's... and that of Lady Gisela, soft and measured. Finally, he saw her beringed hand, as he bent to kiss it...

Then the table seemed to tilt upwards, as his head fell forward. His eyes closed, and a moment later he was asleep where he sat, head resting on his good arm.

For a while Jenna remained where she stood, eyes upon him, until he began to snore. Then she turned away quietly, snuffed out one candle and took another one, to light her way up the narrow stairway to bed.

***

Around dawn Revill woke abruptly, thinking he was back in his chamber at Farthingdown. He stared about in the dim light, before coming to his senses. Stiff, and still saddle-sore from his ride, he sat up with a groan, aware once more of a dull pain in his upper arm. But it was easier than the day before, he thought... he wrinkled his nose, smelling fish. Blearily he glanced aside at his untouched supper and realised his appetite had gone.

A few minutes later, he opened the door to their bedchamber and waited until he heard Jenna's gentle breathing. Striving to make no noise, he sat down by the wall, set his back against it and pulled off his boots. His doublet, however, was a struggle: he got it unbuttoned and freed his good arm, then began work on the other – until there came a stir from the bed, and a gasp.

'Sweet Jesus, Will! What are you doing?'

'I tried not to wake you,' he muttered.

She got up, stumbling about in the gloom. Then there was a spark and a flame, and the candle was lit. Placing it on the floor, she came forward and sat down to face him, pulling her shift about her.

'What am I to do with you?' She breathed.

He made no answer.

'I thought...' she hesitated, then: 'I thought something bad had happened – and not just because you were away longer than you said you'd be.'

'I meant to send a letter,' he said. 'Things got muddled... I should never have gone.' But when she waited, his gaze dropped. He had told himself he wouldn't lie to her again - but how could he not? Whereupon, as her words struck him, he looked up.

'What do you mean, not just because I was away for longer?'

'I mean someone came looking for you - this very morning. And I don't mean one of your old soldier friends - this one looked like he was spoiling for a fight.' She gave a sigh. 'Who have you offended this time?'

In the darkened chamber Revill stared at her, his thoughts leaping - and very soon an image came to mind: of Lewis Turnbull, his face twisted with pain and anger, glaring at him in a dusty stable in Weybridge while Tom Bright held a poniard to his throat.

'There was a bit of trouble...' he began - then he was filled with alarm. Could the man really have come here – and so soon? Surely, he would not yet have learned of Sir Abel's death - and besides, how did he know where Revill

A RELUCTANT ASSASSIN

lived? Now, anger surged up. That Jenna could have been threatened, or even put in danger...

'Trouble, you say.' She let out another sigh, then brought her palm up and pressed it to his face. 'Who would have guessed that?'

Slowly, he reached up to take her hand in his. 'I'll deal with it,' he said. 'I had no inkling he would come here. And you shouldn't have to bear this-'

'Who would come here?' She demanded, cutting him short. 'And how do you know it was the one you think?'

'Well, in truth I'm uncertain. Will you tell me what he looked like?'

'Good clothes... wide chops and a reddish beard – and a sneer. Called me his *sweetness*, only he said it like an insult. He asked if you'd returned home - and when I told him no, he wouldn't believe me. So, I defied him to search the house for himself, and he got angry.' She frowned, remembering. 'He had another fellow with him too, big and shaggy as a bear... looked as if he'd like to break me in two. They went off in a huff.'

Drawing a breath, Revill let go of her hand, then said: 'I need you to leave here for a while – and I mean today. Will you do that?'

'Are you in jest? You've only just got back,' she retorted. But seeing he was in earnest, a slight frown appeared. 'Will... in heaven's name, what have you done?'

'I'll tell you, soon enough,' he answered. 'But the man you saw will return, and I don't want you here when he does. Will you go and stay with someone, until I come to fetch you? Can you go to the haberdasher?'

'I suppose I can,' Jenna replied, after a moment. 'Mistress Stephens is a good friend... I could take my work with me.'

'Good...' he let out a sigh and fell back against the wall.

'But first, hadn't you best finish undressing and get into bed for a while?' She added, with a sigh of her own. 'I'm getting cold – and so are you.'

Whereupon she kissed him on the mouth and began helping him off with his doublet.

***

By mid-morning, after Jenna had departed for the haberdasher's shop in Lombard Street, he had made his preparations.

There was no rear entrance to the tiny house, and the front door was stout. More, there was food and drink to last for a day or two. Before leaving, biting back the questions she was eager to put, Jenna had inspected his wounded arm and rebandaged it expertly. The pain had faded now, much to his relief - for he knew he faced an attempt on his life. Several times that day he recalled the bitter look on Turnbull's face, back in the stable, as he spat out the words: *Once you'd despatched Sir Abel, I was to despatch you – and I wish to God I had!* It prompted him to recall his own thought that had followed: how Sir Thomas Heneage would want no-one left alive who might speak of his own treachery.

And yet, as far as Heneage knew, Revill believed, he had simply carried out his mission: Sir Abel Stanbury was dead – even if he himself had been an accidental and unwilling party to it. As for what he had learned about the Vice-Chamberlain's affairs and his association with Turnbull and Hugh Stanbury, that was no longer his concern – and besides, it was beyond his control. Though it sobered him when he thought of Lady Gisela and the uncertain future she faced, he could not afford to dwell on it. Just now, he thought of Jenna and the life they had... though that too, appeared clouded in uncertainty.

A RELUCTANT ASSASSIN

One thing he was resolved to do, however: send word to Heneage at Sir Francis Walsingham's house as ordered, informing him that the inspection of Farthingdown Manor had been concluded. By mid-day he had penned a few lines to that effect, found a neighbour's boy who was willing, and paid him to carry the letter.

That done, he took a hasty meal of the cold fish pie and spent time cleaning his sword and poniard; both were somewhat blunted and needed honing with the stone. Then he turned attention to the firearms that were kept in a chest, in the parlour that faced the street.

They lay unused, as they had been since his return from the Low Countries: the old wheel-lock pistol, its butt scarred and blackened from half a dozen campaigns, and his light caliver, its barrel stuffed with oiled rags. There too was his powder flask, and a bag of iron bullets. After unlocking the chest and throwing back the lid, he paused to look down at the weapons and recalled his words to Jenna, the day he had put them away: that he hoped never to use them again. But of course, it was a foolish notion: what Captain of Artillery would think of returning to war without arms? Moreover, what Captain of Artillery would think of never returning to war? What else would he do, if the call came – plead that he was needed in London, to teach trained-bands how to march with pikes?

With a muttered oath of reproach, he reached down and took out the caliver, then the pistol. Soon he was seated at the table in the kitchen, cleaning and oiling both guns. But throughout the afternoon, as he found other small tasks to occupy himself, he had one ear cocked towards the house door. It was locked securely, but of course it could be forced; in an idle moment, he pictured Tom Bright breaking open the one at John Cowley's farm – and the sight of Sir Abel in his night-shirt, holding out his old, jewelled dagger.

He was back at the table as evening fell, with a cup of wine: the last of a small keg of Rhenish he had kept, and which Jenna had left untouched. There had been no visitors, and he began to wonder if he had been too hasty in sending her away. Brooding on the matter, he finished the wine and found himself about to yawn... whereupon a loud knocking on the door made him tense from head to toe.

At once he was on his feet, reaching for the pistol – then realised he hadn't loaded it. Cursing under his breath, he took up his sword, drew it from the scabbard and moved out to the hallway. But he had barely reached the door when there was another knock, followed by a voice.

'Captain Revill? Are you within? It's John Marsh – Alderman Marsh. Do you hear me?'

With a sigh of relief, quickly followed by a moment of irritation, Revill lowered his sword and set it by the wall. Then he was unlocking the door and throwing it wide to reveal a stocky man, hatted and cloaked, wearing a look of pained indignation.

'Here you are, sir – at home and at your ease, so it appears, and no word sent to me about your absence!' The man said. 'Had you forgotten that yesterday was the sabbath, and your presence was expected at the Artillery Field? More than a hundred men of the Shoreditch trained-band standing idle half the morning, awaiting their captain – who never appeared. And where was he, sir? I demand an explanation of you!'

Summoning a rueful smile, Revill made his apology to Alderman Marsh of Bishopsgate Ward, a well-known stickler for duty, pleading a sickness which had laid him low. He was on the point of promising to take the drill

A RELUCTANT ASSASSIN

without fee on the following Sunday, but stopped himself: he did not know if that were possible. Finally, hoping his visitor had been placated, he muttered an excuse and began to close the door... whereupon the other gave a start.

'By heaven – I smell wine on your breath! A sickness, you say?' The Alderman was puffing himself up. 'By the looks of you, it appears to me more like you spent the sabbath drinking!' He gave a sigh of exasperation. 'You old soldiers – you have no shame!'

And with that he turned to take his leave – but was thwarted abruptly.

From the gloom of the unlit street, two figures loomed up. One of them, a huge man, shoved Alderman Marsh aside with ease, sending him hurtling away down Abchurch Lane. He then thrust Revill violently backwards, causing him to fall on his rump, and stepped into the hallway. After him came another man, as familiar as he was unwanted.

'Home at last, eh Revill?' Lewis Turnbull said, closing the door firmly behind him. 'That's well – have you time for a talk?'

TWELVE

What followed was not a talk, of course. It was a short preamble to Revill's imminent assassination – and an opportunity for Turnbull to claim his bitter revenge.

'I heard you performed your task, in the end,' he said, in a bland voice. 'Clumsy as it was. Why you couldn't have despatched that old fool Stanbury within a day or two still remains dark to me.' He shrugged. 'But there it is - and now I have my part to do.'

He was seated at the kitchen table, feet upon it to show command of his victim as well as disdain. Revill, unarmed and silent, was on a stool nearby, while the hired man – the one Jenna had described accurately as being big and shaggy as a bear - stood close behind him. He had bound Revill's wrists at his back and cuffed him about the head twice for good measure. From where he sat Revill smelled his breath, sour as a ferret's.

'Do you have anything to drink before we leave?' Turnbull went on. 'I've a powerful thirst, as no doubt Gadd has too.' He looked above Revill's head. 'What say you, my friend?'

Master Gadd barely grunted a reply. Whereupon Turnbull glanced about, saw the small keg on the floor and pointed to it. 'What's in there?'

'It's empty,' Revill replied. His face bore no expression, but his mind was busy. He knew his chances were slim, even non-existent - but if a sliver of one arose,

A RELUCTANT ASSASSIN

he would seize it. It would hardly be the first time he had acted without hope of success.

'He says it's empty,' Turnbull said. 'Too mean to share it, perhaps... will you look, Gadd?'

The hired man moved aside, took up the keg and shook it, then dropped it.

'Ah, well...' His master sighed, before a thought struck him. 'Is your paramour away?' He asked Revill, with a thin smile. 'The pretty fox-haired callett... I was delighted to meet her yesterday.' The smile became a lewd grin. 'I even had a notion of spending a little time with her, after we finish our business. I'll bet she's a joy, with her charms laid open to view, eh? Would you care to describe them?'

Revill drew a breath and watched him.

'Or must I speculate?' The other went on, savouring the effect of his taunts. 'By the Christ, I believe my breeches are tightening at the very thought.'

And still, Revill watched him.

'But then again...' with a sniff, Turnbull lost his smile and slapped his gloved hand down. 'There's work to do, and we waste time.' Removing his legs from the table, he sat up. 'Our journey will be short, but my man will watch your every move,' he added, his eyes on Revill's. 'And your mouth will be covered... no sense in trying to call out.'

He stood up and glanced at Gadd, who seized Revill roughly and hauled him to his feet.

'I'd like to know where we're going,' Revill said quietly. 'Call it idle curiosity.'

His answer was to be spun around, as Turnbull's giant henchman put a strip of linen about his mouth and pulled it tight. As he was tying it Turnbull's gaze fell upon the pistol and the caliver, where Revill had laid them.

'Expecting me, were you?' He asked. 'What a disappointment it must be, to find yourself caught so easily. Downright careless, I'd say.'

He nodded to Gadd, who put his hands at Revill's back and steered him out into the hallway. Turnbull followed, but paused when he saw the sword leaning against the wall. 'Speaking of carelessness...' he gave a snort of laughter. 'Why did you lay that aside? Were you loth to scare your visitor away? That fusty old precisian... I hope you didn't hurt him, Master Gadd. You were a trifle harsh with him.'

He stepped past Revill to open the door – and in that moment, everything changed.

The moment was fleeting, but Revill would know it later as one that saved his life. He was being manhandled towards the door as Turnbull threw it wide - whereupon there came a glare of lantern-light, and a loud voice called out.

'Halt and yield! You are arrested!'

In an instant, hope sprang in his heart – and here was his chance. Swerving aside, he banged his forehead against Gadd's massive jawbone with full force. Then he kicked him on the shin, following it with a knee to the thigh. And even before Gadd staggered, he had whirled round to face Turnbull, who was reaching for his sword...

'If you draw blade, I will shoot!'

Turnbull froze, his hand on the rapier's hilt. Revill peered past him and saw three men, alert and half-crouching. Two appeared to be watchmen, holding lanterns and oak billets – but the other was Alderman Marsh, levelling a pistol at Turnbull's chest. Seconds flew by - until there came a bellow worthy of a raging bull, and a shape charged past Revill.

A RELUCTANT ASSASSIN

Before the Alderman and his companions could react, Gadd had thrown himself at them - but his assault was thwarted. Even as he crashed into them, ignoring the blow one managed to deal him with his billet and downing the other one, there came a lurid flash of flame and the spluttering roar of Marsh's pistol. The ball struck the big man in his side, passing through his innards. He lurched and let out another bellow… though this one tailed off to a great sigh, before he fell to the cobbles. And there he sat, blood seeping through his jerkin.

Revill, tied and still gagged, stumbled out into the street, his eyes flickering from Gadd to Master Marsh who stood rigid, the smoking pistol in his hand. Before anyone could speak, however, there was rapid movement from the doorway. Revill barely had time to whirl round before a figure darted by him, running full tilt. And at once, he knew that Turnbull was gone: disappearing into the dark, his footfalls fading as he turned the corner.

After that, things went eerily quiet.

'I'm very glad to see you, Master Marsh,' Revill said after a moment, but all that came out of his mouth were muffled noises. Whereupon, in something of a daze, the alderman stepped forward and began to untie the strip of linen.

'What did you say?' He enquired, as the cloth came away.

'It doesn't matter.'

Revill breathed deeply, and looked round to see one watchman helping the other to his feet. The man's lantern had fallen and gone dark, he was winded but otherwise appeared unhurt. In shocked silence the men gazed at Marsh, then at Revill, and finally at their assailant, sitting upright and wheezing like an ox.

'Alderman, would you oblige me by freeing my hands?' Revill said.

Somewhat shakily, Marsh glanced at him before bending down and placing his pistol on the cobbles. Then, as Revill obligingly turned his back, he drew out a pocket-knife and cut the cords.

'In the Lord's name, what happened here?' He muttered.

'You know how old soldiers are,' Revill replied, massaging his wrists. 'They make enemies.'

The alderman's brow creased. 'Well, it's clear enough that you do.'

He was looking down at Gadd... who lifted his head briefly, then keeled over on his side. There in the street, under the gaze of the officers, he let out a groan... and died. Blood pooled about his body, glistening in the lantern's glow.

'Who were they?' Marsh asked hoarsely. 'This one, and the one who fled? He looked like a gentleman.'

'Looks can deceive,' Revill replied. Now that the excitement was passed, he felt a sudden need for a glass of something strong.

'I'll have to report it,' the alderman added. 'To the officers of Candlewick Ward – this isn't my bailiwick.'

'Must you?' Revill said, after a pause. 'Wouldn't that bring you a deal of trouble?' And when the other gave a start: 'Don't misunderstand me. You probably saved my life, and I'm in your debt – but you killed the fellow. The other got away before anyone saw him, I'd say. We only need deal with the body. I could testify that this one broke into my house intending to rob and murder me, and you shot him in my defence - or even self-defence. These officers...' He indicated the watchmen. 'They can testify to that, can't they?'

A RELUCTANT ASSASSIN

'Lord above...' Marsh returned his gaze. 'You're a brutal fellow, Revill.'

'I'm thinking of you,' Revill told him. 'If this man has kin – and more, if the officers of this ward aren't satisfied - there could be consequences...'

'He's right, master.'

The watchman who had borne the brunt of Gadd's attack spoke up quickly. Pointing to the dead man with his billet, he added: 'This was a villain down to his boots. And you acted well - any one of us could have been killed.'

But the alderman wasn't happy; *a fusty old precisian*, Turnbull had called him, and the description was not inapt.

'Whoever he was, he should have a proper burial,' he objected.

'Well... perhaps I could oblige there,' Revill put in, as an idea occurred. And when the others turned to him: 'Suppose I make the arrangements? You can return to your duties, and I'll make report to the proper authority. In fact, I'll say I shot this man when he broke in. I've a pistol indoors, that will furnish the evidence.'

A silence fell. The two watchmen, he saw – who had clearly been called in a hurry by Marsh, and embroiled in an affair not to their liking – were in favour. He waited.

'What about the other one?' Marsh asked, with a frown. 'The one with the sword?'

'I didn't see anyone else,' Revill replied. 'Did you?'

His question was for the watchmen, who exchanged looks. Finally, one of them eyed Marsh and said: 'It's the shortest way out of this pickle, isn't it?'

For a moment, it looked as if the alderman would protest... then it passed. With a sigh, he took a step away from Gadd's body. At the same time, a door opened a little way along the street and a head poked out. It was followed by another: anxious faces, peering into the street.

'Let me deal with it, Master Marsh,' Revill said, not unkindly. 'As I said, you've saved my life. The least I can do is save you having to account for...' he paused. 'For what happened.'

Another silence followed, before at last the man lowered his gaze. Stooping, he picked up his pistol and then, to the surprise of the others, held it out to Revill, butt first.

'This is the piece that was fired,' he said. 'Take it, and do what you must. I don't wish to see it again.'

Wordlessly, Revill took the weapon. Whereupon without further word, Marsh turned and walked away. The watchmen waited until he had disappeared around the corner into Candewick Street, then faced Revill.

'If you'll help me remove this,' he said, with a nod towards Gadd's corpse, 'there's a shilling in it for each of you. I'll wash the street down later.'

The two exchanged glances once more, then nodded.

***

By the following morning, all was done. The body of a vagrant criminal, name unknown, had been delivered for burial to the sexton at St Lawrence Poultney, where money had changed hands. As for reporting the death to the officials of Candlewick Ward: that promise Revill allowed to slip from his mind. Just now he faced two immediate concerns: firstly, that he and Jenna should move lodgings that very day – and secondly, that he had to find Lewis Turnbull and kill him.

There was no choice. The man was now an enemy, who would doubtless try again to carry out the order he claimed he was given by Heneage: to put an end to Revill's life. He had failed in two attempts and made a narrow escape, but would be determined not to fail a third time. Revill did not intend to allow him that chance.

A RELUCTANT ASSASSIN

But one thing was clear to him, as he left the house and made his way through the busy city to Lombard Street: he could not tell Jenna. She would be appalled by his intent and would try to dissuade him; though he had resolved not to lie to her, he would have to be evasive. That morning he had formed a notion to seek out a man who might know where Turnbull could be found, which involved a ride out of London.

On arriving at the house of the haberdasher, however, he found himself unwelcome.

'Jenna has gone to market with my wife,' Jonas Stephens said. 'And I'm a busy man. If you want to leave a message, I'll see she gets it.'

Revill let out a sigh. He and the haberdasher – a man with an annoying sense of self-importance – had never got along. Stephens had no time for soldiers, or even ex-soldiers, and considered Revill reckless and unreliable. He stood impatiently in his shop, awaiting a reply.

'I'll pen a message if you'll loan me ink and quill, and a scrap of paper,' Revill said finally. Perhaps it was better this way, he thought, though she would need help in finding new lodgings. And there was the matter of finding a carrier to move their possessions...

'Loan you ink and paper?' Stephens said, wrinkling his nose. 'Did you mean donate them?'

'I meant neither,' Revill answered sharply, his patience short this morning. 'I'll pay you here and now, and I'll leave money for Jenna. My letter will explain what it's for.'

'It sounds urgent,' the other said. 'Then, trouble always seems to follow you, does it not?'

'Shall we say sixpence for your pains?' Revill suggested, as if he hadn't heard. 'And I'll need to ask one further service of you: that when Jenna is gone from here, she can leave her new address with you. I have to be out of London for a while.'

'Indeed?' Master Stephens raised his eyebrows. 'Soldiering business, is it?'

But when his visitor merely waited, he went off to get paper and ink.

An hour later, having been home briefly to gather his belongings, Revill was leading Malachi across London Bridge through the usual throng of people. Arriving on the Surrey side, he got himself mounted and headed downriver, to Deptford.

***

It was almost mid-day when, after passing through Redriff, he drew rein in the little riverside hamlet. The great, grey expanse of the Thames stretched away before him, with the Royal Dockyards a short distance ahead. The place was lively enough, with boats on the river and noise from the dockyard. The man he wanted to see lived – or Revill hoped he still lived – in a narrow street by the Watergate. They had not set eyes on each other for over a year, back in the Low Countries; fraught times, that allowed little opportunity for forming friendships. But then, Elias Rook had no friends, claiming that he couldn't afford them; an occasional intelligencer and recruiter for Walsingham, poorly paid, he was an embittered man. Revill would make an effort to adopt the right means of approaching him.

He dismounted, hungry and thirsty, and led the horse the short distance from the river to a row of low cottages. Not knowing which one Rook occupied, he knocked at the door of the first house and was told that the man he wanted no longer lived nearby. However, at this time of day he would likely be found at the inn by the waterside: the Sea-Hog. And so, a few minutes later, having paid a village boy

A RELUCTANT ASSASSIN

to hold Malachi until his return, Revill pushed open the door of the old tavern and peered through a haze of tobacco smoke.

Heads turned at his entrance: villagers, sailors and fishermen, eying him and his sword with curiosity. Ignoring their looks, he surveyed the large room with its low, blackened beams, and finally set eyes on a hunched figure seated in a corner. At the same moment the man recognised him too - and frowned. Moving slowly, Revill made his way through the drinkers.

'Master Rook.' Glancing around, he found a stool, drew it close and sat on it.

'Bloody Will Revill.' The other glowered at him. 'Why in God's name are you here?'

'I was passing by... seemed to recall this was where you quenched your thirst.'

'Passing by?' Rook sneered. 'On the lookout for a ship, more like. Have things got too dull for you, back in the arms of Sweet Albion?'

'Not for me,' Revill answered. 'Are you waiting on a ship yourself?'

'What is it you want?' Came the terse rejoinder. 'I prefer to drink alone, so if you-'

'Lewis Turnbull - seen him lately, have you?'

To that, the man made no answer. Revill took the time to look him over, noting that he had lost a deal of hair since their last encounter, and what remained was grey like his beard. But the sharp little eyes were the same: watchful, and never free of suspicion.

'I need to find him,' Revill added. 'It's a matter of business.'

'What sort of business would that be?' Rook countered. But at that moment a drawer in a dirty apron appeared at

Revill's elbow and asked him what he would have. He ordered a mug of the house ale.

'The matter is...' keeping eyes on him, Master Rook picked up his own cannikin, took a pull and lowered it. 'The matter is, I'm loth to help you even if I could,' he said. 'You attract trouble - left one man in an alley a while back with his skull broken, or so I heard. My advice would be to take the first vessel that leaves here for France. The field of battle's your natural home, is it not? There's always a need for mercenaries.'

'I'm no mercenary, as you know well enough,' Revill said gently. 'Nor do I seek your advice. I need to find Turnbull – but if you don't know where he is, I'll take my drink elsewhere and leave you to your own miserable company.'

'Why do you need to find him?' Rook enquired, somewhat sharply.

'It's not something I want to discuss – or, not with you.'

'Very well.' The man's sneer was back. 'Then, his whereabouts are not something I want to discuss either. And certainly not with you.'

A moment passed – until to Rook's displeasure, Revill relaxed visibly. He knew this man well enough, and had not forgotten his weakness. Reaching for his purse, he unlaced it from his belt and plonked it on the table between them.

'I'll dice with you,' he said.

The other blinked. 'Will you, now?'

'Best of five throws. If I lose, I'll buy you a mug and leave,' Revill told him. 'You lose, you tell me where Turnbull can be found. I know he's working as an intelligencer, as I know you're Heneage's man down here. If you can't tell me with any certainty where the man is,

A RELUCTANT ASSASSIN

then admit it now and I'll buy you a mug anyway. Is that generous enough for you?'

'We can use my dice,' Rook said, after a moment.

'Oh, no.' Revill eyed him. 'You may say I attract trouble, but I haven't lost my wits.'

A slow smile appeared, followed by a nod. 'As you wish.'

He looked up as the drawer arrived with the ale. When the man set it down, Rook asked him to bring over a bale of dice. Facing Revill again, he said: 'Here's an odd thing: your name was mentioned to me a while back, as it happens. Some people think you could be useful in other ways than firing cannons at town walls. Things being what they are, just now.'

'What – you mean, turn spy?' Revill shook his head. 'I'd rather stab myself.' He paused, then: 'It sounds as if Master Secretary grows somewhat desperate.'

'I said *some think you could be useful*,' Rook retorted. 'I'm not one of them.'

'I'm relieved to hear it.'

'Even though it's a deal less dangerous than fighting Spaniards?'

'I'm done with that, too,' Revill replied. – which prompted a snort.

'You're dreaming, master artilleryman,' the other scoffed. 'Danger will always find you - as it always finds men like you.'

A hand appeared then, to drop a pair of dice on the table. Made of carved bone, they looked well-used but genuine enough. When Rook gestured to him to inspect them, he did so.

'Will you go first?' Revill invited.

Rook took another drink, picked up the dice and shook them in his fist. When he threw them, the score was eight: a five and a three.

Revill took his turn and threw six. In response, Rook threw ten. Revill then threw eleven. His opponent snatched the dice, rattled them impatiently and threw a two.

'Just a pair of eyes,' Revill said – and threw two threes. Rook drew a breath, making no secret of his displeasure… but a moment later it was over. The next throw was four to nine in Revill's favour, followed by a deciding pair of sixes; he had won.

'To the devil with you,' Rook snapped.

Revill waited, until a glowering look appeared.

'Well then, I'll allow that luck has favoured you this time,' the loser said. 'And in more ways than one. You want Lewis Turnbull; you can find him just by walking.'

And when Revill raised his brows:

'He's here in Deptford, and has been since early this morning. Now do I have to stand you that drink, too?'

THIRTEEN

He waited until nightfall before making his preparations.

It had turned cold, with a strong wind coming up the Thames, banging doors and shutters about the village. Otherwise, Deptford had grown quiet, though sounds of revelry drifted from the Sea-Hog. Revill was not far away, having found stabling for Malachi. Throughout the day he had stayed clear of the waterside, buying dinner from a bakery before making his way to Deptford Creek, where he made himself comfortable under a tree. From here he could look downstream to the wild osier beds, or across to the Queen's great palace of Placentia, which she often visited. Though there was no royal standard flying, which was some relief given his business in hand; the fewer people there were around just now, the better.

By evening he was tense as a post, and chilled to the bone. In the dark, he loaded and primed his pistol; the caliver he had left back in London, knowing it would attract attention. At last, he arose, stamped about to awaken his limbs, and buckled on his sword. Then he was walking through the meadow at the rear of the village, past the church and onto Deptford Green, which was bordered by a few small dwellings.

In one of them, a lodging-house kept by a widow named Katherine Pollitt, Lewis Turnbull was lying low while he awaited a ship to take him out of England.

JOHN PILKINGTON

That was as much as Revill had managed to draw from a morose Elias Rook, following their dice-play. And it now appeared that, after the previous day's debacle in Abchurch Lane, Turnbull was heeding the advice Revill had given him back in the stable in Weybridge: to avoid Heneage and return to the continent. He must have left the city at first light rather than face the spymaster, though he had been obliged to seek out Rook to wheedle a small payment out of him. It meant that the man was no longer hunting Revill down – for the present, at least. But it made no difference to his resolve: he had only to think of Jenna, and the way Turnbull had spoken of her – and how the man had brought grief to the house of Sir Abel Stanbury. It had been drilled into him long ago by his stern father: once set upon a purpose, a man does not shirk from seeing it through.

He reached the last cottage in the row and halted. A light showed downstairs, and another one, much fainter, at an upper window. Briefly he felt the butt of the pistol, tucked into his belt and hidden under his short cloak, then without knocking he tried the latch. He was not surprised when it lifted; folk seldom locked their doors in places like this. Stepping into the dimly-lit cottage, he closed the door swiftly – whereupon a female voice from across the room challenged him.

'Here, who are you?'

He took a pace and removed his hat. 'Mistress Pollitt? Your pardon for my intrusion, not to say my late arrival. I was told you had rooms for hire?'

There was a swish of skirts, and a figure rose from beside a table where a candle burned. She was tall, with a mass of hair, and wearing a loose gown of cherry-red taffeta. She came forward, looked Revill over, then put on a sad smile.

A RELUCTANT ASSASSIN

'I keep one room, sir, yet I must disappoint you. It's been taken by another gentleman.'

'Indeed?' Revill smiled in return. 'That's a pity. I've ridden far and am somewhat weary.'

'I'm most pained to hear it,' came the reply. 'If you wish, I can point you to another house, over by the shipyard.'

Revill regarded her, then glanced about the room, his mind busy. He knew that Turnbull, like other shiftless men who often travelled out from Deptford, likely had a regular bolthole in which to stay while awaiting a ship, and many of them preferred places kept by women. There was one such house here that he knew of, kept by an Eleanor Bull, where intelligencers were said to meet – but Elias Rook had sent him here, and he was willing to believe him.

As he had done once that day already, he decided to gamble.

'In truth, mistress, I don't require a bed this night,' he admitted. And when the widow's smile faded: 'I believe I know the gentleman who is above, and have a notion to surprise him. Might his name be Norris... Richard Norris?'

But at that a look came over her face, as hard as a mask.

'I know nobody of that name, sir. I fear you're mistaken.'

'He also uses the name Turnbull,' Revill said.

'That too,' Mistress Pollitt replied, 'means nothing to me.'

She glanced down at his sword, and thence to where the butt of his pistol bulged. A moment passed – but when she opened her mouth to shout, Revill leaped.

'I pray you, be quiet,' he muttered, pressing a hand across her lips. 'I mean you no harm–'

But with a grunt of pain, he broke off, as she sank her teeth into his forefinger - and after that things went badly. She was strong: a seaman's widow, and not unused to brawling. She kicked him, then her hand flew beneath his cloak – and at once she had seized the pistol. Her grasp was clumsy, however: Revill was able to grab her hand and force it aside. Briefly they wrestled for the weapon, until it fell to the floor - and produced an almighty explosion as the hammer was struck.

Revill blinked, half-blinded by the flash. Mistress Pollitt fell back – but the next instant relief swept over him: the ball had slammed into the wall, barely a yard away. Powder-smoke clouded the room… sensing movement, he whirled about and caught the widow's hand before it could reach his eyes. Whereupon they were locked in a new tussle, his opponent gasping as she sought to master him. Her knee came up, narrowly missing his groin - then she yelled at the top of her voice, so close to Revill's ear he was almost deafened.

'Turnbull! Down here!'

But there was no need: the pistol-shot, of course, had already roused her lodger. There was a thud of feet on floorboards overhead, leaving Revill no time to do other than shove Mistress Pollitt to the floor and draw his sword. Stumbling to the foot of the stairway, he managed to reach it just as Lewis Turnbull did, holding a poniard. But as his foot hit the bottom step, Revill's dagger flew up to prick his hand, at which he yelped and dropped the blade.

A moment later he was pinned against the wall, the point of a rapier at his throat.

'This is getting to be a habit with us,' Revill breathed, eyes fixed on those of his enemy. 'But I mean to break it.' He glanced briefly at Mistress Pollitt, who was struggling to her feet… whereupon she sagged, let out a sigh and shook her head.

'By the Christ, Turnbull!' She roared, in a voice worthy of a Billingsgate fish-wife. 'Why couldn't you have stayed in London? And when did you ever bring me aught but grief!?'

***

There was no time to lose: the noise of the shot would bring people. Revill sat Katherine Pollitt down and ordered her to stay silent for five minutes before she answered her door. Otherwise, he added, he would tie her up, gag her and cut her fingers off. And though he knew she didn't believe him, he thought he could get outside quickly enough to be concealed by the dark – with his prisoner.

His prisoner, trussed like a fowl with the sleeves of his own shirt, bare-chested and shivering, sat by the door where he had been put.

'You understand?' Revill demanded, looking down at her. 'Your friend and I have business, that doesn't concern you. Is he worth your trouble?'

'My friend?' The woman glowered at him, then threw a baleful look at Turnbull. 'He was once – no longer.'

'A pox on you, you raddled old whore!' Turnbull cried, twisting his body about. But the bonds held; shifting his eyes to Revill, he cursed roundly.

Mistress Pollitt let out an angry snort and levelled a finger at him. 'Whatever you've done, I hope this man slits your throat, you bastard,' she threw back. 'If I had my way, you'd be-'

'Enough!' Revill raised his hand, the forefinger of which now bore a livid imprint of teeth-marks. Impatiently, he snatched his pistol up from the floor and strode over to Turnbull.

'On your feet,' he ordered, stowing away the firearm. And when the other made no effort to rise he leaned down, seized his shoulders and hauled him upright... as he had done once before, he recalled, in the moonlit gardens of Farthingdown Manor.

'I do my own dirty work, as a rule,' Revill said. 'I don't have a shaggy-haired giant to do it for me. But you'll do the same as you told me yesternight: walk ahead and make no sound, or I'll spike you.' To press home the message, he drew his poniard and jammed the point against his prisoner's ribs. Turnbull flinched and drew breath sharply, but when Revill prodded his bare back, he got himself shakily to the door. Revill leaned forward to open it, letting in a gust of chilly air, before turning to Mistress Pollitt for the last time.

'Whatever's left in his room is yours to sell,' he said. 'He was never here, and nor was I. As you said, his name means nothing to you.'

The widow eyed him, her hands grasping the arms of the chair, but said not a word. And thereafter both men were soon outside, the door closing behind them.

'March,' Revill said, giving the other a shove. Turnbull hesitated, shivering, then began to walk ahead of him across the green – and not before time. As the two of them melted into the dark, voices sounded from the direction of the cottages. Someone banged on a door, which had to be Mistress Pollitt's.

'Stir yourself,' Revill ordered, forcing his prisoner to quicken his pace. To their right, the outline of the old church was visible, before they reached the pathway at the edge of the green. Then they were in the meadow, with Deptford Creek ahead. Finally, by the water's edge, Revill called a halt.

A RELUCTANT ASSASSIN

'There's a vessel, due in from Calais in the morning,' Turnbull said suddenly, half-turning to him. 'I was to be on her when she sails.'

He spoke in a tone Revill had never heard him use before – hurried, and almost plaintive. But then, the reason was clear enough: he expected to die very soon, and was trying desperately to stall.

'Then she can sail without you,' Revill replied. 'Now kneel.'

'There's a good sword and cloak back at the widow's house, plus a gold piece hidden in my hat,' his prisoner went on – but his answer was to be shoved forward on to his knees.

'You know they need men like you?' Turnbull said then, speaking quickly. 'We've no need to remain enemies, you and I. Over in France things are in turmoil, and as for the Spanish-'

'Save your breath,' Revill broke in. Then he drew his sword – and at the sound of steel scraping on scabbard, his victim started like a rabbit.

'You've no need to do this,' he jabbered. 'I was under orders from Heneage... you're a soldier. You must have been given tasks you didn't want...'

'As I recall, it didn't look to me as if you disliked the order,' Revill said. 'You tried hard enough to carry it out.'

'No – listen, your reasoning is at fault! You know I can't disobey Heneage - he doesn't brook failure, as you said yourself. And besides, you're not a murderer!'

'I'm a butcher,' Revill reminded him. 'You said so yourself, remember?'

To that, the other had no reply... and now, it was as if they were back beside the brewhouse wall at Farthingdown, trading insults on another chilly night. To Revill, it already seemed a long time ago. Pushing the notion aside, he raised his sword; he had a mind to use the old Roman thrust, down through the man's left shoulder beside his collar-bone, and thence to the heart. He had seen it done... he steeled himself, tightened his grip on the hilt...

'Mercy!'

Turnbull's terrified cry stopped him dead.

'For the love of God, Revill!' The man's head snapped round, trying to face him in the gloom. 'Show mercy, like a good Christian... I implore you...'

Revill swallowed, as a shiver passed down his spine. An image flew up: of a desperate Spaniard in a dusty street in Axel, begging for his life... *Mercy, señor...* he saw the man's dark eyes, his rough beard flecked with blood... and his strength seemed to run out of him, to soak into the grass at his feet.

He lowered his sword. The wind soughed in the osiers, while in the distance faint lights showed from the Queen's palace... and then a different sound broke into his consciousness.

At his feet, Lewis Turnbull was bawling like a child.

***

He left Deptford shortly before noon on the following day.

In fact, he thought later, he could have left in the early morning; there was no danger now. In return for his life being spared, Turnbull had sworn he would take ship for France and not return. Revill knew he would have promised anything, but it hardly seemed to matter. Having told his intended victim that he would speak with Elias Rook to make sure he kept his word, he was content to let him make arrangements. The last that he saw of the man was his disappearing in the direction of the Sea-Hog, where he would beg a share of one of the rooms the inn

A RELUCTANT ASSASSIN

kept for sailors, before boarding the vessel at the first opportunity.

Revill had walked to the stable and spent the night on straw beside Malachi.

London's East Cheap was roaring that afternoon, as he walked the horse slowly through the press of market folk, passers-by and beggars. Church bells clanged from all sides, out of time and out of tune, while overhead a rain shower threatened. By the time he had reached Candlewick Street and the turning to Abchurch Lane, the first drops were landing on his hat. He urged Malachi as far as his front door... then reined in abruptly.

The door was wide open, and off its hinges.

For a moment he sat in the saddle, his gaze shifting from the broken door to the street, but there was no-one about. Then, as he dismounted, a figure hurried out of the house.

'Revill? By God... when I heard hooves, I thought-'

'Master Burrell?' He was looking at his elderly landlord, whom he hadn't seen in weeks – and one glance was enough to gauge his alarm. 'What was it you thought?'

'That they were back!' The old man slumped in relief. 'The rogues - do you see what they did? I wouldn't believe it, when one of your neighbours sent his boy to tell me. But now...' He broke off, shaking his head.

'What have they done? Revill asked sharply. He glanced through the doorway and saw something lying on the floor - whereupon his heart thudded.

'You'd best come in and see,' Burrell began, but Revill was already pushing past him – to stop abruptly. It was a counterpane, that the day before had lain on his and Jenna's bed, and it had been roughly torn. His eyes rose to the stairway, where other items of linen lay scattered.

'The rest of the place is... well, it's in mighty poor array,' Burrell said from behind him.

Without turning round Revill walked into the kitchen and knew then that the entire house had been ransacked.

'When did it happen?' He asked the landlord, as he shuffled in.

'Yesterday, sometime. Seems there was a brabble here the day before... a pistol-shot was heard.'

'You mean, someone's forced their way in here in broad daylight?'

The other gave a shrug. 'Looks that way.' A frown appeared. 'From what I hear, the brabble was outside your door. Is there something you ought to tell me?'

Revill made no reply. His mind was spinning, as he thought of Jenna... had she been back to the house? Whoever had done this, he was sure, was looking for him - and when they failed to find him, they appeared to have vented their frustration on the property. Everywhere he looked, things were broken and thrown about. His caliver was gone, of course, as would be anything else of value. But it wasn't Turnbull who had done this, since he had already fled to Deptford... whereupon realisation dawned.

Heneage still wanted him dead.

'What are you going to do?' Burrell enquired, in a surly tone. 'Some of these things are mine... or they used to be. I'll want compensation.'

'Has anyone else been here since it happened?' Revill demanded, swinging round.

'You mean your doxy?' The old man gave a sniff. 'I wouldn't know.'

'I must leave you,' Revill said, with a hard look. 'I'll return later to pick up anything that's worth saving.' He turned to the door, but Burrell stayed him.

A RELUCTANT ASSASSIN

'I've heard other things,' he muttered. 'Seems the Watch was called... I've no wish to see my house let to lawbreakers.'

'Then allow me to satisfy you – for I and my companion will be quitting it today.' Reaching for his purse, which was now almost empty, Revill unlaced it and shook out a few coins. 'Will this settle the rent, and your compensation too?'

Master Burrell lowered his eyes, surveyed the silver, then gave a nod. And with that they parted, Revill striding from the house to where Malachi waited patiently in the rain. As he swung himself up into the saddle, he caught sight of a streak of something on the cobbles: a trace of Gadd's blood, that he had failed to wash away. Then, with luck the rain would finish the task for him.

A moment later he had turned his mount and was heading for the far end of the lane, and the turning into Lombard Street.

***

His first sensation, on arriving at the haberdasher's house, was one of overwhelming relief: Jenna was there, and had not been to Abchurch Lane after all. His next reaction was of growing irritation: Jonas Stephens, it seemed, was highly displeased.

'What is she to think - what are all of us to think, the way you come and go at your pleasure?' He asked haughtily. 'She's been at sixes and sevens ever since she read that letter you left. That woman deserves better, I'd say.'

They stood in the back room of the shop, while the man's wife carried on their business at the front; Jenna, who was above, had only now been told of Revill's arrival. He waited in silence until she hurried down the stairs, to arrive with a look of huge relief. But there was no greeting. She stopped, drew a breath, then looked at Stephens.

'I suppose you have private business,' the haberdasher said frostily, with a glance at each of them in turn. To Jenna he added: 'You know where I'll be, if needed.'

She nodded, then lowered her eyes. Once they were alone Revill went to her, but she barely embraced him.

'Where did you go, Will?' She looked up at him anxiously. 'Or must I ask once again - what have you been doing?'

'I've settled some business,' he answered, feeling weary on a sudden. 'The man who came to the house won't trouble us again – and no,' he added quickly. 'I didn't harm anyone.'

'But... your message. I thought-'

'I'm still not free of it, yet,' he broke in. 'I need to take some time, decide what to do.'

'You look dog-tired,' she said, after a moment. And when he barely shrugged: 'You should go somewhere you can rest. Why don't you seek out Tom Bright?'

'Well, I could...' he gazed at her, then stiffened. 'You haven't begun to look for another lodging, have you?' And when she shook her head: 'Abchurch Lane has been broken into... there's likely nothing left worth saving.'

She sighed and closed her eyes.

'You wouldn't feel safe as long as you're with me, would you?' He said then – to which her silence was answer enough.

'Well, mayhap Master Stephens is right,' he went on, with a bitter smile forming. 'To say I only bring you trouble, that is. He seems to have appointed himself your protector.'

'Then let him think it,' Jenna said, with another sigh. 'Mary is my friend, and she wants me to stay here. Now

A RELUCTANT ASSASSIN

their children are up and gone, there's room. I can do my broidery work, and help with the shop.' She met his gaze, and when he made no answer: 'It's best for now, is it not?'

'I suppose it is,' Revill allowed, after a moment.

'Go, then,' she said, suddenly sharp. 'I'll wait until you return… however long it may be.'

And with that she hugged him tightly, pressing her body to his. They kissed, before she pulled away, turned about and waited for him to leave.

FOURTEEN

When he arrived at Tom Bright's tumbledown lodging in Dowgate, he found that his old sergeant was as good as his word: he appeared to have been drunk since they parted. Revill managed to rouse him, before hauling him out into the noisy street where he hailed a passing water-carrier, bought a jugful and poured it over Bright's head. With a roar and a curse Bright sat down heavily, then looked up at him through bleary eyes.

'Jesus, Captain! Did you have to do that?'

'I had to let fly at someone,' Revill said shortly. 'It may as well be you.'

'What the devil are you doing here?'

'I came to beg a place to sleep. Your floor will serve as well as any other.'

With a groan, the little sergeant got to his knees, then on to his feet. 'What are you varlets looking at?' He snarled, eying a couple of youths who had stopped to enjoy the entertainment. When they merely laughed, he started towards them – only for Revill to catch him by the collar of his jerkin.

'I need a drink, and so do you,' he said. 'I mean a proper drink, to wash away the swill you've been downing. You stink like a sutler's beer-tent.'

'You mean, you're paying?' Bright turned about, water still dripping from his hair.

A RELUCTANT ASSASSIN

'I suppose I am. Now I think on it, I need to eat something too.'

They eyed each other: Bright, still unsteady, squinting up at his old Captain with a growing look of concern. Revill, his expression softening, released him.

'The Three Cranes in the Vintry?' The sergeant suggested.

Revill nodded.

At the old inn by the waterside, with dusk falling, he spent most of what remained of his money on a beef supper, washed down with the best ale. Finally, with Bright almost restored to full sensibility they were able to take their ease, Revill paying a penny for a small pipe of tobacco. He drew in the first, welcome draught, unable to remember when he had last enjoyed a smoke. He exhaled, and found his old sergeant's eyes upon him.

'Things haven't fadged too well since you got home, then?' He enquired, in a casual tone.

'You might say so,' Revill replied.

'And you need a bivouac. Has Jenna thrown you out?'

'Not exactly. But just now, I'm as good as a vagabond.'

'Well, you know you've a bed with me. It's not much, but-'

'We've known worse,' Revill finished.

He took another puff, then leaned back against the wall. The inn was filling up with evening drinkers from the wharves, along with a sprinkling of upright citizens. Finally, he eyed Bright and began to talk. And gradually, unhurriedly, he told his tale and was relieved to do so: all that had happened since he had got home and learned of Turnbull's visit, up until his return from Deptford. When he finally ended with an account of his leave-taking at the haberdasher's, the sergeant took a pull from his mug, lowered it and let out a long breath.

'Jesus, Captain. You've took risks, right enough.'

Revill barely shrugged.

'I should have cut Turnbull's throat back in that stable when I had the chance.'

'With hindsight, you're probably right.'

'So - what's your next move?'

'For once, Tom,' came the reply,' I haven't a notion. Though I suspect my presence at the Artillery Field next sabbath won't be welcome.'

'In truth, there's nothing for me here either,' Bright said, after a moment's thought. 'I had a hope my landlord's daughter would still be on offer after I go back from Farthingdown, like she used to be. But hear this: she's getting married – to a bricklayer!'

'She could do worse,' Revill observed, taking another puff on the pipe.

The sergeant gave a snort. 'Like marrying a soldier?'

A few moments passed, before Bright added: 'Young Lord Willoughby's in France now, fighting for the new king. Henri of Navarre's no king at all as yet, since he can't even enter Paris.'

'So I've heard,' Revill said, without much interest.

'Seems he begged our Queen for help,' the other went on. 'Trying the old French charm, with flowery letters and such. One thing she can't resist is flattery – and now she's sending troops. But then, she don't want Papists for next-door neighbours.'

'There are plenty over in Ireland,' Revill observed dryly.

'You know what I'm saying, Captain,' Bright retorted. 'There's work needs to be done over there. If the Catholic League keep a hold over France, there's a route through to England for the Spanish, straight across the Channel. They

A RELUCTANT ASSASSIN

wouldn't even need to build another armada – just a fleet of flyboats.'

'So that's the way your mind moves, is it?' Revill found himself frowning. 'Back to the battlefield? I thought you'd had enough of it.'

'So did I,' the sergeant admitted. 'But what's a man to do? I can't lay bricks.'

They were both silent then, brooding on the inescapable fact: that like most soldiers, they had little else to fall back on but their fighting skills. Finally Bright picked up his mug, drained it to the last and plonked it down.

'A gentleman like you might have choices, Captain,' he muttered. 'I don't.'

Revill made no reply. His thoughts drifted briefly to Devon, and the family farm: to his elderly, half-blind mother and his older brother. Robert Revill held the land now, and held it fast. There would be no welcome for the wayward son who had gone off to university on a scholarship, then thrown it all away to become a captain of cannons.

'You're serious, then?' He enquired, turning his gaze upon his sergeant. 'You'd cross the Manche, and offer your services to Willoughby?' And when the other hesitated: 'He'd take you, of course - you're one of the best cannoneers he had.'

'Some say you were the best captain of gunnery,' the other returned.

'Masters of slaughter is all we were,' Revill murmured.

'From what you've told me, you're lucky to have escaped slaughter yourself,' Bright retorted, not liking that description at all. 'If Heneage has marked you for a doomed man, it'll make small difference whether Turnbull's here in England or not. Some other varlet will be given the order, and come looking for you.'

'I know that,' Revill said. 'It's why I left Jenna where she's safe and came here.'

'In which case, Captain - at risk of going about in circles – I'll ask again: what's your next move to be?'

'I must attend Heneage myself – face to face. I see no other course of action.'

Having exhausted the last shred of tobacco, he laid the pipe down. The idea had been brewing for some time, he knew – and now he had said it aloud.

'You mean, stick your head in the lion's mouth?' Bright frowned. 'That's madness.'

'I won't run away,' Revill said sharply. 'Which going off to France would mean, when all's said and sifted. Besides, I'd not be safe, even there. I know too much about Master Vice-Chamberlain, and his greedy little scheme to profit from Sir Abel Stanbury's death.' He drew a breath, then: 'And more, I feel I owe that old man something. He deserved better – as does Lady Gisela. Even if her knave of a son will inherit, after all.'

A moment passed, before Bright let out a sigh. 'Well, then... you'd best sleep on it, at least,' he grunted. 'Tomorrow-'

'Tomorrow I'll feel the same, Tom,' Revill broke in.

'I know that,' the sergeant answered testily. 'I was about to say, tomorrow we might put our heads together and find a way for you to get near enough to Heneage to speak with him. You surely can't go to Sir Francis Walsingham's house – his men would seize you, and you'd end up in irons.'

Revill met his gaze, then managed a nod.

And later that night, on a rough straw pallet on the floor of Tom Bright's dingy little chamber, the notion stayed with him before he finally drifted off to sleep.

***

A RELUCTANT ASSASSIN

In the morning, he was abed far longer than he intended. Wearied from the events of the past days, he awoke in some confusion, before looking about and finding Bright's bed empty. Rousing himself, with the din of the street in his ears, he moved to the window and looked out towards the Thames, just visible over the rooftops... whereupon the remembrance of his predicament descended on him like a sack of coals. He moved to a stool, cleared aside the clothes that had been strewn across it, and sat down heavily.

All in all, he realised, nothing had really changed: whatever he did he was in thrall to Heneage, and a marked man to boot. His sister Katherine and her young husband were the weapon the Vice-Chamberlain still held, and could hold as long as he wished. And though he was determined to confront the man, he saw little chance of success.

He dressed slowly, and was on the point of venturing out when the door opened and his sergeant came in, looking surprisingly cheerful. Revill threw him a bleak look.

'I've got news,' Bright began. 'It seems the Queen's off to Richmond Palace today, by the royal barge. She'll likely be hawking this afternoon, on the hill, and-'

'Why in God's name should I care?' Revill broke in sourly. But when the other's face fell, he looked away. 'Pay me no mind... haven't woken up yet.'

'You need a breakfast,' Bright said. 'Some days, the landlord's daughter stands me a bowl of porridge and a crust, but she's not here.' He paused, looking his old Captain up and down. 'And yet, if you'll let me finish what I was saying, there's a ghost of a chance for you to carry out your plan – on Richmond Hill. Do you see?'

'See what?' Revill asked, not understanding.

167

'Heneage will be there with the Queen, of course, along with other Privy Councillors,' the little sergeant told him. 'Walsingham's still sick, so…'

'Hawking?' As the penny dropped, Revill's expression cleared. 'You mean, I might catch Heneage off guard?'

'With a bird on your wrist, and wearing a different suit of clothes, why couldn't you?' Bright said. 'By the time he's recognised you, you can say what you have to say.' He put on a wry look. 'Not that I've changed my mind: you'll still be putting yourself in mortal danger. One word from him, and the Queen's guards will come running.'

'True, but…' Revill breathed a sigh. 'It's the only course. I'm in your debt again, Tom.'

'That you are,' the other agreed. 'But for now, you'd best make ready. It's a fair ride out to Richmond.'

***

The morning passed, far too slowly for Revill's liking.

Money was his chief difficulty, his purse being all but empty. Somewhat to his surprise, however, Bright still had some shillings left from the payment he had received when they last parted. When assembled, the sum was enough for Revill to get Malachi out of the stable, pay for his food and purchase a serviceable hat, doublet and short cloak from a fripperer's stall in West Cheap. Thus attired, and having taken a mid-day meal with his sergeant at an ordinary on Fish Street Hill, he took his farewell at the crossroads by Thames Street, where they had parted four days previously.

This time, however, their discourse was taut, Bright having lost his affable demeanour of the morning. It must have appeared to him, Revill thought, as though the two of them had little chance of meeting again.

'I still say it's madness,' the sergeant muttered, as they stood in the busy street among the press of traffic on foot

A RELUCTANT ASSASSIN

and on hoof. As Revill held Malachi's rein, Bright ruffled the old warhorse's mane, then prepared to take his leave.

'You know where I am,' he said, with an effort. 'And I expect that loan to be repaid.'

'You won't be off to France just yet, then?' Revill enquired, with a wry look.

'I might... then again, I might not.'

With that he turned abruptly and walked off into Stockfishmonger Row, shouldering his way into the crowd.

Revill turned away, put foot in stirrup and got himself mounted.

The ride to Richmond took over an hour, given the muddiness of the roads: there had been another shower in the night. He passed unhurriedly through Newington, Clapham and Wandsworth, crossed the stream and turned south-west towards Roehampton. Finally, with the wooded hills of Combe Park on his left, he reached the old village of Richmond on the Thames, dominated by its great royal palace. He had calculated that the Queen's barge should have arrived there before now, likely presaging one of Elizabeth's prolonged stays at one of her favourite residencies. The day being fair, it seemed likely enough that she would ride to hawking on the hill close by, as Bright had predicted. He recalled the little sergeant's face that morning: eager to please, even though this journey was as fraught with danger as any Revill had undertaken. The difference was, it was no battlefield he faced, but an assembly of courtiers and nobles, eager to gather about their Queen when she took her pleasures. Hawking was prominent among them... which meant Revill had to equip himself with a suitable cover, and quickly.

He was unfamiliar with Richmond, but it was not difficult to find a falconer in a country village surrounded by suitable terrain. Having tethered Malachi, he ventured into a couple of inns and asked the topers, claiming that his own bird was out of sorts today. It was not long before he was directed to a John Belford, who kept a number of falcons and might be willing to hire one out. In his new attire, with hat pulled low, he led his mount to the man's cottage, and was relieved to find that, thus far at least, his luck was holding.

'I can loan you Salome,' the falconer said, looking his visitor up and down. 'She's the only one I have left to spare. There's no shortage of gentlemen showing up, once the Queen is come: strangers, eager to borrow a bird so they can trail after her. I see you're one of them.'

Revill eyed him: a stooped old countryman with straggly white hair, wearing a well-worn gauntlet of thick leather on his wrist. They stood in his tiny garden which was almost filled by a mews made of withies, where his avian charges were kept. There were perches in the open, but all were empty save one, where a large female falcon gazed unblinkingly at him.

'She's a beauty,' Revill said, nodding appreciatively. 'And I'll take good care of her.'

'You'll need to,' the other replied, in a dour tone. 'She's no patience with novices...' a frown appeared. 'And where's your glove?'

'Ah...' Revill forced a grin and spread his hands. 'I fear I've I mislaid it... had too much business this morning. Can you assist me?'

The oldster sighed and jerked his head towards the house. 'Come along, then... I dare say I can find one.' He paused, then: 'You won't keep Salome out if the rain starts, will you?'

It was more of an instruction than a question. Fortunately, though it was a long time since he had flown

A RELUCTANT ASSASSIN

a bird – back in Devon, he thought – Revill was not ignorant of the sport.

'Of course not,' he answered. 'I'll treat her as if she were my own. Her name is… Mab. And doubtless there will be some cover on the hill when the company gathers.'

'Doubtless,' the other replied, in a somewhat mocking tone. 'But as for *when the company gathers*, you're a little late. I saw riders going out hours ago.' He squinted up at the sky. 'So - we'd best get our business done, eh?'

It was concluded quickly enough. Having been paid his fee without a quibble, half to be refunded when the falcon was returned, Master Belford's manner eased somewhat. Mumbling as he moved about the house, he equipped his customer with a stout gauntlet of ox-hide and a hood for the bird. When they returned outdoors, the old man took Salome on to his wrist, hooded her and carried her out of the garden into the lane, where Malachi waited. Once Revill was back in the saddle, he bent down to receive the splendid falcon on his own gauntlet. The bells on her jesses tinkled as she changed position, but she was docile enough; she seemed to sense the presence of both horse and rider, ruffling her plumage slightly. Taking the rein in his free hand, Revill nodded thanks to her owner.

'She's eager to hunt, right enough,' Belford said. 'If you bring anything down worth eating, I'll not refuse a brace of fowls for my supper.'

Then he stepped back while Revill eased Malachi up the lane, finally turning away from the village where the ground rose. And quite soon, Richmond Hill was ahead.

Thereafter, as he rode up the narrow path, he tensed further with every step.

It was quite easy to find the hawking party: almost too easy, he thought. After passing through trees where a few people were strolling, and thence to open ground, he heard distant shouts – and looked up sharply, to see two or three large falcons floating high above on the breeze. As he watched, one dropped suddenly, speeding down upon its hapless prey. From the trees at his back, he heard other birds squawking in alarm before flying away. Lowering his gaze, he peered ahead – only to rein in abruptly.

Two men in royal livery, wearing swords and carrying halberds, were blocking his way.

'Who are you, and what do you want here?' One of them asked, stepping forward smartly. The other followed, the two of them taut with suspicion.

'Good afternoon,' Revill said, forcing a cordial smile. 'My name is... Croxton. And as you see, I'm here to join Her Royal Majesty at the hunt. I hope I'm not too late?'

The two eyed him, noting his appearance as well as Salome, who sat motionless on the gauntlet.

'Croxton?' One of them shook his head. 'Not a name I've heard. Are you invited?'

'Of course, I am,' Revill lied. 'By the Vice-Chamberlain himself, no less. I trust Sir Thomas is already abroad?'

'I believe so,' the other man replied. He had relaxed somewhat, although his companion had not. Setting the base of his halberd on the ground, he stood astride belligerently.

'We need more than words... sir,' he said, forcing the last word out. 'There's always danger to Her Majesty, and it oft comes in disguise. What's your relation to the Vice-Chamberlain?'

'My relation?' Revill took a breath: he had no way of knowing how much these men knew about Heneage. He had to bluff, which was a risk... but then, the day before, he had not expected to get even this close to the man who had ordered his death. Once again, he had no other choice but to take risks.

'You will know of Sir Thomas's daughter, Elizabeth?' He said, adopting a haughty tone. 'I'm her suitor – and I dislike your tone, fellow. You'd do well to show a little courtesy to one who's a firm friend of the Heneage family.'

The belligerent halberdier frowned. 'Well, as I said, your name's unknown–'

'As I am also close to Lady Anne Heneage,' Revill broke in, ignoring the reply. 'You'll recall she's the daughter of Sir Nicholas Poyntz – an old friend of my father's. That's Sir Jasper Croxton, in case you didn't know. He has six hundred acres, down in Devonshire.'

A pause followed, in which Revill knew everything hung in the balance: not only his chances of accosting Heneage, but his possible arrest as an imposter – or worse, a spy. He had already come to the end of what he knew about the Vice-Chamberlain's relatives; maintaining a frosty stare, he waited.

Mercifully, the strategy was adequate. The two men looked at each other... and finally a nod passed from Revill's interrogator to his companion.

'Your pardon, sir,' he said, somewhat gruffly. 'We have our orders, and no man can be too careful in these times. Will you ride on with our blessing, and-'

'And forget the insult I've received here?' Revill snapped, concealing his relief. 'Well, as of now I'm uncertain... perhaps you'd better give me your names, eh?'

At that, the more easy-going of the two gulped, and swallowed loud enough to be heard. But the other forced a contrite look and made his bow.

'I'm Barnes, sir,' he said. 'And this is Wilmot. Once again, we ask pardon. I can do no more than ask your mercy and wish you a good afternoon's hunting. Now, will you ride?'

'Well, I will,' Revill said, after a pause. He glanced from one man to the other, then shook the reins. 'And since the day holds fair for sport, I'll forget what's passed between us… but not your names,' he added. 'Just in case, that is.'

Whereupon, with a look of disdain, he urged Malachi forward as the two guards stood back; they even made their bows as he passed. He could almost hear Tom Bright laughing and applauding his performance, as he rode steadily onwards, now catching sight of riders in the distance.

Above him the falcons still swooped, while Salome roused on the gauntlet. Soon he heard voices ahead, and saw men on foot, russet-clad with feathers in their hats and hawks on their wrists: royal falconers, one of whom turned at his approach.

Drawing a long breath, Revill eased his horse forwards towards the party, his eyes peeled for sign of Sir Thomas Heneage.

And a short while later, he would find him.

FIFTEEN

The Vice-Chamberlain was not a hawking man, nor even a known lover of the English countryside - but wherever he might be, he was seldom far from the seat of power. The seat of power, for her part, was some distance from Revill as he rode up, concealed among the royal ladies and an attendant flock of richly-dressed courtiers. There were other riders scattered about, along with a sprinkling of servants and men with dogs on leashes. Despite the clouds that loured overhead it was a cheerful affair, likely a prologue to an evening of hearty eating and entertainment. Revill walked Malachi unhurriedly towards the falconer who had noticed him. Taking him for an important guest, the man at once made his bow.

'You're most welcome, sir... have you ridden far?'

'Not far...' Revill's eyes swept the terrain. 'Is there good sport today?'

'Slow at first, but we hope for better,' the other replied – whereupon he looked at Salome, and a slight frown appeared. 'I know that bird,' he said. 'Is it not one of John Belford's?'

Stuck for an answer, Revill hesitated. 'It is,' he answered finally. 'My bird being sick of the frounce, and being treated by my own falconer, I was obliged to borrow Mistress Salome here.'

'Is it so?' The man was eying him keenly. 'And would you care to tell me how your bird is being treated?'

'With powdered rock-alum,' Revill told him, managing to dredge up a memory from his youth. 'Some swear by aqua fortis, do they not? But my man knows better, as a rule.'

Whereupon he waited... to be rewarded by the sight of the royal falconer relaxing; he even smiled. 'Then he's one after my own heart, sir,' he said. 'I would use rock-alum myself.'

At that, Revill too relaxed – but only slightly. Peering ahead, he asked the falconer if he had seen Sir Thomas Heneage, adding that he was eager to pay respects to him. The man nodded and pointed towards the group of milling riders.

'He's somewhere over there, sir... he was one of the first to ride out, following the Queen.' The man's grin broadened. 'She barely stopped to take any dinner, but was eager to be up on the hill the moment her barge docked. Tomorrow, I hear she'll hunt stags. There's hardly a man who can keep up with her!'

To which Revill nodded, before urging Malachi towards the falconry party. But he was too tense – which Salome sensed and twitched slightly. Riding slowly over the grass, he soon reached the stragglers: mainly young gallants sitting their saddles, more concerned with banter and gossip than with hawking. One or two of them glanced at him as he passed, without speaking. Liveried servants moved about, some carrying leather mugs and even stoups of wine. When one approached Revill, he waved him away...

And then, he saw Heneage.

He too was sitting his horse, dressed in a good hunting suit and in conversation with another nobleman, though he carried no falcon. A little over a dozen yards separated him from Revill - and already he could hear the familiar voice,

A RELUCTANT ASSASSIN

the man's languid tone. Slowing Malachi almost to a halt, he searched for words - then remembered why he was supposed to be here. Letting go of the rein, he drew the hood off Salome's head, unwound the jesses from his wrist and lifted his arm high with a bowling motion. At once the falcon spread her wings and leaped, soaring to a good height in seconds and finally hanging high above, gliding as if she were weightless. Revill paused long enough to watch her, then lowered his gaze - to stiffen abruptly.

Heneage had ceased his conversation, and was riding towards him at pace.

'You... how dare you come here!'

His mouth tight, eyes blazing, the Vice-Chamberlain rode determinedly up to him until their mounts almost touched heads, reining in at the last second. His own horse, a fine black gelding, jerked aside; Malachi barely flinched. Whereupon Heneage leaned forward in the saddle, lifted a gloved hand and pointed.

'You're a ghost, Revill,' he said, in an icy tone. 'You're already dead – twice over. And at a word from me, the job will be finished – this time without fail!'

'Indeed, sir? I pray, who will you send this time?' Revill replied. 'It won't be Lewis Turnbull. Last I saw, he was weeping on his knees in Deptford before fleeing the country.'

Heneage drew a sharp, angry breath - and now at last, battle was drawn. Revill was surprised at how calm he felt. If nothing else, he thought briefly, he could vent his anger at this man, even if it were the last thing he did. A feeling came over him that he soon recognised: the cold, eerie calm of close combat, when a soldier knew that every approaching second might be his last...

Then an idea flew up from somewhere, and he decided to use it.

'But the matter is, sir,' he said, meeting Heneage's fierce gaze, 'I fear you're mistaken - or so I'll be telling anyone who draws near. My name's Croxton, and I'm come from France – an emissary from Lord Willoughby, with tidings for the Queen's Council. There are several of them here, are there not? I expect Her Majesty herself will want to be informed-'

'Oh, no – that will not succeed!'

Heneage snapped the words out, but gave a swift glance to either side: fortunately for his sake, there was no-one close by. Facing Revill again, he lowered his voice.

'Do you forget who I am?' He muttered. 'And do you truly imagine I'd let you get within twenty paces of the Queen? I only need call out to have you arrested as a would-be assassin – and I'll provide enough detail to make it stick! You're for the nearest lock-up, where you'll meet with an accident, or a fatal disease… either will do.'

'I'll still say you're mistaken,' Revill answered. On impulse, he turned to the servant he had waved away but was still within calling distance and shouted loudly.

'Over here, fellow! I've changed my mind about the drink!'

Heneage jerked his head, stifling a curse, but to no avail: the man had already turned towards them. Revill waved him forward, then faced his adversary again.

'I mean to make a noise and a fuss – sir,' he hissed, allowing his anger to surface at last. 'I'll pick a fight with someone - mayhap I'll even threaten you. Then when the guards take me, I'll blab that it was all your doing: that I'm your hired assassin who killed Sir Abel Stanbury in Surrey, here to demand my fee. Before they stop my mouth, I'll let it out that you're set for a handsome payment from Hugh Stanbury, when the Farthingdown lands are sold - and that you're a scheming varlet who's plotting to succeed

A RELUCTANT ASSASSIN

Walsingham. I could say you're drunk on power, so sick with greed you're half-way to madness...'

He stopped himself, breathing hard, as the servant with the jug of wine reached them.

'Will you take claret, sir?' The man asked politely. 'Or I can have someone bring a stoup of Rhenish?'

'Claret's fine - good man,' Revill replied, with an effort. 'Though I seem to have mislaid my hunting cup... do you have a mug about you?'

The servant nodded helpfully, gesturing towards one of his fellows, and said he would fetch a cup at once. Revill watched him go, then turned deliberately to Heneage. He expected the Vice-Chamberlain to be frothing with rage... but he paused.

The man was eying him with a mixture of anger, helplessness... and something else. Could it even have been wry amusement?

'By God...' letting out a long sigh, Heneage slowly shook his head. 'I heard things about you, from Turnbull of all people - things I dismissed. But you bettered him from the start – or so I've gathered. He lied to me, of course, but his excuses were hollow. He knew I wouldn't swallow them a second time – which is why he fled.' He paused, and a hard look appeared. 'And you let him go in Deptford, when you could have killed him? Why?'

Revill met his eye. 'Because, as I told you weeks ago, I'm a soldier and not an assassin. Yet you chose to force me into that role, by the cruellest means...'

He paused, remembering: remembering conversations back at Farthingdown: with Turnbull, with Leonard Ashman... and with Lady Gisela, in his candlelit chamber. His mouth taut, he looked up to find Heneage wearing an expression he found hard to judge.

JOHN PILKINGTON

'By heaven, Revill...' the man sighed again. 'What in God's name shall I do with you?'

Revill gave him no answer. His anger had lessened slightly, though it was far from spent. It occurred to him briefly that, had he harboured a real desire to kill this man, he could do it here and now, with ease: overpower him and stab him to the heart before anyone noticed - and hang the consequences. To any onlooker, for the present they appeared merely as two gentlemen - one a holder of high office, admittedly, the other a stranger – engaged in casual conversation. At least, that was what the servants had assumed... he looked round and saw the bearer of claret hurrying up with a pewter cup, which he offered at once.

'I thank you...' Revill took the vessel, allowed the man to fill it, then raised it to Heneage with a bland look. 'Will you partake, Sir Thomas?' He enquired. 'Do share with me.'

'I think not,' the Vice-Chamberlain said quietly.

He half-turned to the servant, who had been looking expectantly at him, and was clearly on the verge of telling the man to make himself scarce. But to his irritation, Revill stayed the fellow, fumbling for his purse. Producing a threepenny piece, he tossed it down. Catching the coin deftly, the man made his bow and went.

'Courage is one thing, Revill,' Heneage said, as the man drew out of earshot. 'Bravado is another... but plain recklessness can get you killed.'

'You have that power, sir,' Revill allowed, matching his dry tone. 'As you made clear when I was summoned to Seething Lane and given a mission, the true cause of which I did not understand. Now I do understand – and more, the death you bespoke took place, if not in the way it was ordered. But as you said to me that same day: a drowned Spaniard is as good as one who's been shot – you

A RELUCTANT ASSASSIN

remember? Hence, a target who dies of a seizure serves your purpose as well as one who's met with a fatal accident... is that not so?'

But Heneage was uncharacteristically silent. Distant shouts drifted on the air... Revill glanced up to see that Salome still hovered above, at what falconers called *high mountee*. He lowered his gaze, to find the Vice-Chamberlain staring at him through narrowed eyes.

'Do you know what a *carnifex* is, Revill?' He asked.

'If I recall my Latin correctly, the word means *executioner*,' Revill replied, feeling a frown forming... then he gave a start, even as the other nodded.

'That's what I had in mind for you,' Heneage said. 'A useful bondsman, no stranger to dealing out death when required. Not one of the sort of oafs Turnbull hires, nor some ex-foot-soldier... nor even a brute of a turnkey who cares naught for life. No – a gentleman, an officer who can pass among the high-born, with the brains to pick the right moment.'

He looked away briefly – but when he returned his gaze, Revill was wary.

'But then... now that I've allowed you to have your say, you'd have to admit that the case is unaltered,' the Vice-Chamberlain added smoothly. 'Do you follow?'

Revill breathed in, then tried to answer levelly.

'If by that, you mean that you still hold my sister's life in your hands, like a sword that hangs above both our heads, then I will admit it,' he said. 'And yet...' his voice rising slightly, he added: 'Back in Seething Lane, you told me that my task was *a once-and-for-all-mission, to be well rewarded*. Do you recall that?'

Heneage appeared to ponder the matter. 'I may have done so,' he allowed. 'Though I don't remember using those words.'

'What, then - do you want me to beg?' Revill retorted. 'Is that it – that I should beg for the life of my innocent sister? Very well – I will beg!'

With that, he fell silent. It was all to no avail, he thought bitterly: this was a man with no conscience, and little interest in anything but power and its trappings. Briefly, he found himself wondering how Malachi managed to remain so calm; Henaeage's gelding, he sensed, was growing restless. He looked away, towards the falconry party, and saw that they were now a good deal further off. Following his gaze, the Vice-Chamberlain looked round, and muttered something under his breath. Then he turned to Revill... who raised his eyebrows. He had expected the worst, and was even considering a rapid flight – even taking a ship somewhere - but something in the other's manner stayed him.

'Let me ease your mind,' Heneage said. 'Your sister is safe – for now. Even her Papist husband is safe – for now. But you, Revill, are not. You know perfectly well that, at a word, I can have you taken captive and prevented from telling what you know. Soon afterwards, you'd die in some rathole of a prison, and no-one would bat an eye - nor even know who you were, since your tongue would be cut out. Even your faithful sergeant will have lost track of you by then... and your pretty Cornish broiderer, too. Did you think I knew nothing of her?'

In taut silence, Revill waited.

'And yet, if I had other tasks for you...' the other put on a thin smile. 'Tasks other than executions, that is... if I did, would you continue to serve me?'

Revill frowned – and then the penny dropped.

'You mean, go as an intelligencer - an eavesdropper and a snooper?' He breathed. 'Or a gaol-louse, perhaps, to befriend prisoners and then inform on them?' His anger

A RELUCTANT ASSASSIN

rose as he spoke. 'Or do you see me as one who lurks at harbours, asking for tidings as to what ship is due, and who was on the last one... buying sailors drinks, and wheedling tidings from them as they get soused?' He drew breath, then added: 'You want me to replace Turnbull, is that it? Well, I say no! I'm a soldier – I serve the Queen's Majesty, and none other.'

'Excellent,' Heneage said, after a short silence.

Revill met his gaze, and blinked.

'That could serve me well,' the other went on, as if talking to himself. 'It's as a soldier you shall go – to France, that is. Matters move apace there, and reports can barely keep up. Artillery will soon be in demand, to mount the sieges when they come – as they doubtless will. The new King has his sights on Paris, of course.'

The man's thin smile was back. 'Are you game for returning to the field – Captain?' he enquired. And when Revill made to reply: 'For it's as a captain – even of artillerymen - that you could operate, under a cover. In truth, it's only now that the idea has fully taken hold of me - an excellent notion.'

In spite of himself, Revill was dumbfounded. Where there had been only darkness, he saw a chink of light... but as he pondered the matter further, unease rose again.

'Then, you still want me to spy,' he said flatly. 'On whom – my fellow officers, or my commanders? Even Lord Willoughby – a man for whom I'd lay down my life?'

But to his displeasure, Heneage was almost enjoying himself. Briefly he patted the neck of his mount, which stamped its foot impatiently, then waved a hand in dismissal.

'What nonsense you talk, Revill. I would merely ask for despatches from you – not concerning the enemy, of course; that's a matter for the Queen's commanders in the field. I speak of rumours that may fly about: disgruntled ensigns, mercenaries who talk of going over to the Spanish... even secret Papists. They exist, of course, even in the army. But you know well enough what I speak of.'

The Vice-Chamberlain managed a smile... and seeing Revill lost for an answer, he startled him by tugging the rein suddenly and turning his horse.

'Think on what I've said – and think hard,' he said. 'But don't take too long – and remember, I yet hold your life in my hands, as I do that of your sister. Send me notice of your decision here at Richmond, saying you're preparing to join Willoughby's army in France. In which case, you'll receive word from me later.'

And with that the Vice-Chamberlain put heels to his mount's flanks and rode off, back in the direction of the Queen's party. As he went, he half-turned in the saddle, raising his voice. 'Shall we say tomorrow?'

And he was gone, the rump of his black horse disappearing in the distance.

Revill sat stock-still in the saddle, trying to arrange what had just occurred into some sort of order... and failing. He was still in the same spot when Salome dropped like a stone from the sky with a plump gamebird in her talons, to let it fall beside Malachi's feet. He had barely time to lift his arm, where she settled calmly upon the gauntlet as if nothing at all had happened.

But it had.

SIXTEEN

Two weeks later, on a blustery November morning, Revill and Tom Bright stood on the Legal Quays, a short distance downriver from London Bridge. The waterside was bustling, as the Long Ferry made ready to depart for Gravesend. Once there, the two of them would board ship, joining a party of troops bound for Dieppe. In Dieppe, Revill would oversee the unloading of a small number of culverins and demi-cannon before assembling his company for the march inland. In his pocket were written orders from the Queen's Council, for him to join Lord Willoughby's forces.

There was no order from Sir Thomas Heneage: only a verbal understanding, that, alongside his military duties, Will Revill would take pains to observe his fellow officers in the field, and report on their trustworthiness. It was suggested that he might employ a false name, if required. Moreover, should the need arise, he might be called upon to remove certain parties who were deemed to pose a serious risk to the Crown's interests. The Vice-Chamberlain had provided him with a sum in advance, to remind him of his debt.

In short, Revill was still the Vice-Chamberlain's *carnifex* - his occasional executioner. For in war, especially in the heat of battle, Heneage had reminded him on the single, brief occasion they had met since their encounter on Richmond Hill, anything was possible: a bullet that went astray, a careless gunner, a poorly-timed explosion... even a collapsed bulwark. A man could die a hundred different ways - and no-one would speak of murder.

Tom Bright, muffled against the cold, was sniffing the breeze suspiciously.

'It'll be a rough crossing, Captain,' he grumbled. 'I don't like the sea... if things go badly, I'll be throwing my breakfast up over the side, and no mistake.'

'Think of France, Tom,' Revill said, relieved to be diverted from darker thoughts. 'Think of the wine - and the women, if you like. Back in the Low Countries, you often said you'd like a posting there - now you've got it.'

'Aye, just as winter's drawing close,' Bright muttered. 'Does it snow over there?'

Revill ignored him and glanced about. Passengers were already embarking, clambering down the stone steps to the ferry, where the harassed master tried to get them in order. Apart from the human cargo there were dogs, sheep and even a heifer to keep under control. Finally, the sergeant lifted his heavy pack off the quay and shouldered it.

'Did you make your farewell?' He asked, in a casual tone.

He meant Revill's farewell of Jenna, who had chosen not to come down to see him leave. She would remain at the haberdasher's until he returned, she had promised. The house in Abchurch Lane was now let to another tenant, Jenna having been there with Jonas Stephens to salvage what possessions were worth saving. She had no idea, of course, when Revill would come back; the possibility that he might not come back at all had not been mentioned.

'I did,' he told Bright. 'She's settled where she is.' He drew in a breath of cold air. 'What of you? Was the landlord's daughter sorry to see you go, after all?'

A RELUCTANT ASSASSIN

'Well now, I believe she was,' the little sergeant replied. 'Though the wedding to her bricklayer is still set.' He gave a shrug. 'Still, you know how it'll be, once we're in France. A man forgets things, soon enough.'

Revill almost smiled, knowing Bright as he did. But for himself... he grew thoughtful again. He could never forget Jenna, whatever happened – nor his family. He had sent letters by carrier to Devon, to his brother and to his sister, telling them he was going to war again. To Katherine's message he had added a warning of possible danger, though he had no notion how she might act upon it. The threat sat in his mind still, harsh and immoveable: Heneage's power to force him to carry out acts he might abhor.

But with an effort he thrust such concerns aside, for he had no choice. Soon he would have a different family to care about: his cannoneers, who put their lives in his hands and trusted him to do right. Though there was little to look forward to in the coming days but hard marching on muddy roads in wind and rain, hauling guns from one place to the next, a part of him almost relished it: the strange kind of freedom that campaigning brought. There would likely be mayhem to follow, he knew – yet there would be laughter, borne of the camaraderie of soldiers far from home. He forced himself to think on the business in hand... and on a sudden, remembered something else: that as hoped, he would no longer be available to attend the inquest in Weybridge, into the death of Sir Abel Stanbury. His thoughts strayed briefly to the fateful sojourn he had passed there, and to his last sight of the Master of Farthingdown Manor: a sight he would never forget. Whereupon he realised that Tom Bright, sergeant of gunnery, was addressing him, and forced himself to return abruptly to the present.

'I said are you ready, Captain?' He said loudly, touching him on the arm. 'If you don't stir yourself, they'll shove off without us.'

Revill looked down the steps, to see that they were indeed the last to leave. Whereupon, hefting his own pack, and his new caliver in its shiny new scabbard, he followed Bright down to the covered longboat, now a noisy, seething mass of people and animals. As he clambered aboard, he took a last look behind at the great city. His sergeant, meanwhile, had pushed his way to a bench and was demanding that people move aside to make space.

'Soldiers of the Queen, going to fight for Her Majesty against the Papists,' he announced. 'Where's your respect? Where's your pride?'

Coming up behind him, Revill glanced around as someone shouted from close by, to receive an answering cry from the quayside. Ropes were thrown, oars clattered, and a general hubbub arose, a chorus of farewells from passengers to those who stood above. The boat lurched, and a stiff breeze coming upriver almost blew his hat from his head.

'Why so glum now, Captain?'

Bright was frowning at him, gripping the edge of a seat to steady himself.

'I'm not glum,' Revill told him.

Defiantly he sat down, gazing at the choppy surface of the Thames: his passage out of England. How long it might be before he saw it again, he could not know.

'He's not glum,' Bright muttered to himself.

Then he snatched at his own hat before the wind could take it.

Printed in Great Britain
by Amazon